MANDIE
AND THE
TRUNK'S
SECRET

MANDIE
AND THE
TRUNK'S
SECRET
Lois Gladys Leppard

BETHANY HOUSE PUBLISHERS
MINNEAPOLIS, MINNESOTA 55438
A Division of Bethany Fellowship, Inc.

Library of Congress Catalog Card Number 85-71474

ISBN 0-87123-839-X

Published by Bethany House Publishers
A Division of Bethany Fellowship, Inc.
6820 Auto Club Road, Minneapolis, Minnesota 55438

Printed in the United States of America

For My Son
Donn William Leppard
That rootin', tootin' cowpoke boy,
Now grown so big, handsome, and tall;
Life's most wonderful pride and joy,
And God's most precious gift of all.

About the Author

LOIS GLADYS LEPPARD has been a Federal Civil Service employee in various countries around the world. She makes her home in Greenville, South Carolina.

The stories of her own mother's childhood are the basis for many of the incidents incorporated in this series. This is her fifth book.

Contents

Chapter 1 / Cleaning Up the Attic

Mandie squirmed in her chair in front of the headmistress's desk. She and Celia, her friend, had been called to the office—again.

Miss Prudence Heathwood, the tall, elderly headmistress, and her sister, Miss Hope, ran The Misses Heathwood's School for Girls, a boarding school where Mandie and Celia were students.

Miss Prudence looked sternly at the two girls. "You, Amanda, will not be allowed to participate in the school play," she said. "And, in view of your complete disregard for the school rules, I believe it is necessary for you both to be further disciplined."

The girls looked at each other, not knowing what to expect.

Miss Hope Heathwood, a little younger than her sister, sat to one side, watching the proceedings but saying nothing.

Miss Prudence cleared her throat and continued. "If you two had not insisted on running around after curfew looking for noises in the attic, none of this would be necessary," she reminded them. "This discipline is not only for your good, but also for the good of every other young lady in school here. We must have compliance with our rules. Is that understood?"

"Yes, ma'am," Mandie replied, flipping her long, blonde hair behind her. Then cautiously, she added, "But if we hadn't investigated the noises, we wouldn't have found that poor retarded girl, Hilda, in the attic."

"That is beside the point," the schoolmistress said firmly. "You must learn to do things within the rules." Miss Prudence sat straight in her chair behind the desk, occasionally glancing at her sister. "How that runaway managed to hide in our attic so long, only the Lord knows," she said.

"At least now she's getting some medical help at the sanitarium," Mandie said as respectfully as she could.

"That's enough," Miss Prudence snapped. "I have heard enough of your excuses. I am hereby ordering the two of you to begin the task of cleaning up the attic. I have asked Uncle Cal to assist you, but you are to sacrifice your morning free periods each day until the job is completed. You two will work while the other girls are enjoying their leisure. Is that understood?"

"Yes, ma'am," the girls said together.

"Very well then," Miss Prudence replied. Rising, she motioned to her sister, Miss Hope. "I'm putting you two completely under the supervision of Miss Hope. You will answer to her at all times on all questions. And let me tell you one thing. You two had better remember that. There is to be no more disobedience in this school or your parents will have to find you another school to attend." She turned to Miss Hope. "They're all yours, Sister. See that they live up to the rules," she said, hurrying out of the office.

Miss Hope pushed a stray lock of faded auburn hair into place and sat down behind the desk. "Now, young ladies, I'm sure we won't have any problems," she told them. "If we all live according to the Good Book, everything will be fine."

"I'm going to try real hard, Miss Hope," Mandie promised.

"Me, too," Celia added.

"I do hope you both remember your promises," Miss Hope said. "Now, about this chore of cleaning up the attic." She paused to clear her throat.

"Miss Hope, please tell us about all that stuff in the attic," Mandie begged. "There's so much furniture up there, and boxes, and trunks, and all kinds of things. How do you clean up an attic?"

Miss Hope laughed. "Now that's a good question," she said. "I suppose Uncle Cal can clean up with a broom and mop, and you girls can sort everything out. Maybe put everything of one kind together. You know, if there are clothes in several drawers or boxes, put them all in one spot. Arrange all the books in one place, and so on."

"Then we have permission to open anything up there?" Mandie asked.

"Why, yes. You may open anything in the attic," Miss Hope said.

Mandie's blue eyes grew wide, and the two girls looked at each other.

"Where did so much stuff come from?" Celia asked.

"It's mostly things the former owner left here when my sister and I bought this place. We've been here about forty-five years, but I don't think we've put much in the attic," the schoolmistress told them.

"Forty-five years?" Mandie gasped.

"Yes, about that long. The house was probably twenty years old when we bought it. The lady who owned it was a widow. Her daughter got married and left her alone. She didn't want to live here in this big place by herself, so she sold it to us and went to live with some relatives," Miss Hope explained. "We bought some of her furniture because she couldn't take it all with her. She told us to throw out anything we found in the attic, but we've never really cleaned it out. Most of that stuff up there is not ours."

"Didn't she ever come back for any of it?" Mandie asked.

"No, I don't think we ever saw her again. In fact, she must be dead by now. She was up in years then," the schoolmistress replied.

Mandie wiggled impatiently in her chair and smiled at Celia.

Celia glanced from her friend to Miss Hope. Apparently Miss Hope was not in any hurry to get the cleaning done.

"Well, when do we begin?" Mandie asked.

"You sound as though you're in a hurry," the schoolmistress said.

"We might as well get it over with," Mandie said, "so we can have our free periods for other things."

"I admire your enthusiasm, Amanda," said Miss Hope.

Mandie smiled. " 'Nothing like paying a debt and getting rid of it,' my father always said. And we do owe the school this work because we broke the rules."

"I'm glad you think that way, Amanda," Miss Hope said. "Some girls who have to be penalized for their wrongdoings seem to think we owe them something. I can see your father was a good man."

"My father was a wonderful man, I miss him so much."

Mandie replied with a catch in her voice. "And he died so young . . ." Mandie bit her lip. Then turning to her friend, she added, "And so did Celia's. I suppose that's why we're such good friends. We understand each other."

"Right, Mandie," Celia's green eyes glinted with a touch of sadness.

Miss Hope fumbled with pencils on the desk, looked down at her hands, and then looked squarely at Mandie. "Do you know your father's people very well, Mandie?" she asked.

"Oh, yes, Miss Hope." Mandie brightened. "I have so many wonderful Cherokee relatives. My grandmother was full-blooded Cherokee, you know, but my father never told me for some reason. I didn't know about it until my father died. Then Uncle Ned, his old Indian friend, came and explained everything to me. He told me about my father's brother John, too. I had never even heard of him. But dear old Uncle Ned helped me get to Uncle John's house in Franklin."

"What about your stepmother?" Miss Hope asked.

"Well, you see, I thought my stepmother was my real mother until I went to Uncle John's house. Uncle John found my real mother for me and then the two of them got married," Mandie explained.

Miss Hope leaned forward. "I didn't know all that, Amanda," she said. "I knew your mother, you know, when she went to school here."

"My mother went to school here, too," Celia said, pushing back her thick auburn curls. "Our mothers were friends. Mandie's grandmother told us about it when we went to visit her."

"Yes, I remember your mother very well, Celia," Miss Hope said. "Tell me, dear, how is your mother? Is she adjusting to the loss of your father?"

"I'm not sure, Miss Hope," Celia replied, twisting her fingers in her lap. "You know I haven't been back home to visit since I came here, and Mother doesn't write very often."

"I'll send her a note, Celia, and inquire about her health," the schoolmistress promised.

"Thank you, Miss Hope. I was worried about leaving her at home alone, but she insisted that I come on to school the day after my father's funeral," Celia said, her voice quivering.

"I know, Celia," Miss Hope said, sympathetically, as she rose from her chair. She flipped open the watch she wore on a chain around her neck, then added, "Now, young ladies, as soon as I can find Uncle Cal and set up this cleaning schedule, I'll let you know. But I believe right now it's about time for you to go to the dining room for your noon meal."

The girls stood up.

"Thank you, Miss Hope. I promise to do my best," Mandie told her.

"And I do, too," Celia added.

"That is all I can ask. Now run along," Miss Hope told them.

No talking was ever allowed during mealtime, so as soon as Miss Prudence dismissed everyone, the two girls ran all the way up the stairs to their room on the third floor of the boarding school.

Puffing for breath, they burst into their room and collapsed on the bed, laughing.

"Now we have permission to unlock that trunk we found Hilda beating on," Celia said.

"Right. Miss Hope said it was all right for us to open

anything in the attic," Mandie said. "I sure am anxious to see what's inside that trunk."

"Me, too," her friend answered.

Mandie sat up quickly, pushing back her thick blonde hair, which she now wore loose. "But not anxious enough to break any more rules," she said.

"I'm not either," Celia echoed.

"I'll tell you what," Mandie suggested. "If you catch me breaking any more rules, or about to break any, will you remind me of what happened to us the last time we did such a thing? I don't want to get suspended from school again."

"I will if you'll listen to me, Mandie," her friend agreed, "and if you'll do the same for me."

"It's a promise," Mandie said. "I guess we'd better get going. It's time for our class. I hope we can start cleaning up the attic before too long."

"And I hope whatever's in that trunk is worth losing all our free periods for," Celia told her as they descended the stairs for their history lesson.

"Even if it isn't, I guess we deserve the punishment," Mandie said.

"But I have a feeling there's something exciting hidden in that trunk," Celia said.

Chapter 2 / The Locked Trunk

The ten o'clock curfew bell had already rung. All the lights were out. Mandie and Celia, still dressed, sat on the window seat in the darkness of their room.

Mandie stared out the window. "It's about time for Uncle Ned to come," she told her friend. "I'd better go down to the yard."

"Mandie, why didn't you just tell Miss Hope about Uncle Ned's visits so you wouldn't have to sneak out to see him after everyone is in bed?" Celia asked.

Mandie quickly turned. "Oh, no, Celia!" she said emphatically. "I don't think Miss Hope and Miss Prudence like Indians."

"I suppose a lot of white people are like that," Celia agreed. "But I don't see why."

"Well, I don't either, but I'm not taking any chances. Uncle Ned is my father's friend. He promised to watch over me after my father went to heaven. I don't want anything to stop me from seeing him. And rather than take a chance on telling anyone, I'd rather meet him this way," Mandie explained without taking a breath.

"I understand, Mandie, but please be careful. I don't

want you to get into any trouble," Celia said. "Give Uncle Ned my love."

"I will, Celia. Don't forget to stay by the window where I can see you from the yard. And close that window in a big hurry if you hear anyone coming," Mandie reminded her.

Celia promised she would, and Mandie slipped out into the hallway and down the servants' stairs to the kitchen. Sliding the bolt on the back door, she stepped outside, then ran around to the side of the house where she could see Celia watching from their bedroom window.

Mandie stood in the light of the full moon, watching the shadows of the huge magnolia trees for her old friend. He was usually on time.

Suddenly, she heard a low bird whistle, and she whirled to see Uncle Ned coming toward her.

Mandie ran to meet him. "Uncle Ned!" she exclaimed, grabbing the old Indian's wrinkled hand.

Uncle Ned stooped to hug her tight. "Papoose, sit," he said.

Moving to a bench in the shadows below the opened window, they both sat down.

"I have some exciting news, Uncle Ned," Mandie began. "Remember that girl, Hilda, that Celia and I found hiding in the attic? Remember how we told you that she was beating on an old trunk with a poker trying to open it?"

"Yes, Papoose," the old man answered. "Put sick Papoose in hospital."

"That's right, Uncle Ned," Mandie said. "Well, as our punishment for wandering around after ten o'clock at night, Miss Prudence has ordered Celia and me to clean the attic during our free periods."

The old Indian looked closely at her. "Papoose not open trunk and get in more trouble?" he asked.

"We have Miss Hope's permission to open anything in the attic. We have to sort everything and make it all neat and clean. So Celia and I are going to open that trunk and see what's in it," she told him.

"What Papoose do with what Papoose find in trunk?" he asked.

"That depends on what it is," Mandie replied. "It might be something interesting. Then again, it might just be some old clothes. Only I don't know why anyone would lock old clothes up in a trunk."

"Papoose must be good," the old man warned her. "If find important thing, must tell Miss Head Lady."

"Not Miss Prudence, Head Lady, as you call her. Miss Hope has been put in charge of Celia and me. We have to answer to her," she said.

"Then Papoose must tell Miss Head Lady Number Two," he said. "Papoose must not make more trouble. Jim Shaw not like. I promise Jim Shaw I watch over Papoose while he go to happy hunting ground."

Mandie sobered quickly. "I know, Uncle Ned." She put her arm through his and squeezed it. "I know my father would expect me to live right. I want to be a good person like my father was. I promise to behave," Mandie said, smiling at the old Indian. "Besides, I love you, too, Uncle Ned."

"Papoose dear to heart," the old man assured her.

Mandie sat up straight. "Uncle Ned, did you bring any messages from my friends back home?"

The old Indian smiled broadly. "I bring message from doctor son, Joe," he said. "He come to Asheville with Dr. Woodard soon."

"Oh, that's a *good* message," Mandie said excitedly. "Are Joe and his father going to stay at my grandmother's house?"

"He say he bring white cat see Papoose," the old Indian told her.

"Snowball? Then he must be going to stay with Grandmother because that's where Snowball is," Mandie replied. "Remember Mother couldn't find him when she brought him on the train to see me? Then after Mother left, there was Snowball, sitting on Grandmother's door-step."

Uncle Ned laughed.

"And remember how he got into my baggage when I came back to school from Grandmother's? Celia and I found him under the bed in my room," she said, laughing. "He's a smart cat!"

"White cat have own mind," Uncle Ned agreed.

"Any other messages?" Mandie asked.

"Cherokees at Bird-town and Deep Creek send love, too. They say Papoose hurry back home."

"Tell them all I love them, too, Uncle Ned," Mandie said with a smile. "As soon as I can get a holiday from school I'll be back to see them. I miss everybody so much."

"John Shaw and Papoose's mother want Papoose stay in big house in Franklin," he said.

"Oh, I will, most of the time, but I want to really get to know my other relatives. I'm proud to have Cherokee kinpeople. I'm so glad God made me that way," Mandie said.

"Cherokee proud of Papoose. God know how to make us all just right, Papoose," he replied.

"I know, Uncle Ned."

The old man rose from the bench. Mandie, holding his hand, stood by his side.

"Must go now. Papoose go back. I watch," he told her. "I come see Papoose next moon change."

He bent to hug her, and Mandie kissed his withered old cheek.

"Don't forget, Uncle Ned. I'll be waiting for you," she said. "And please tell everyone I send them my love."

"I tell, Papoose. Now hurry," Uncle Ned said.

Mandie, glancing up at Celia standing by the window above, ran across the grass to the back door. Turning to wave good-bye to the old Indian, she slipped inside the house, shot the bolt across the kitchen door, and made her way back up to her room.

Celia met her at their door.

When Mandie had closed the door softly behind her, she blurted out the good news. "Celia," she said excitedly. "Joe is coming to see me!"

"Oh, I'm so happy for you," Celia replied. "When?"

"I don't know exactly," Mandie said, "but Uncle Ned said 'soon.'"

"Did you tell Uncle Ned that we had to clean up the attic, and about that trunk?"

"Yes, and I promised him we wouldn't get into any more trouble," Mandie said.

The two girls slipped out of their dresses and picked up their nightgowns lying across the foot of the bed.

"Let's not forget to keep that promise, Mandie," Celia said, pulling her nightgown over her head.

"Celia, please keep reminding me of that. I really do want to behave. I want to be the kind of girl my father would be proud of," Mandie said, as she sat down on the side of the bed.

"I know what you mean, Mandie. That goes for me, too," Celia told her. "We'll just have to keep checking on each other."

"Agreed," Mandie said. "Maybe Miss Hope will let us know soon when we're supposed to start on the attic."

A few days later Miss Hope called the girls to her office where Uncle Cal, the school's old Negro servant, was waiting.

"This won't take a minute," the schoolmistress told them. "I've talked to Uncle Cal here and explained what's to be done. You two can begin on the attic during your free period tomorrow morning. Uncle Cal will sweep and mop the place this afternoon, so it won't be so dirty to work in. Then he will unlock everything—all the wardrobes, chests, and so on."

The two girls exchanged glances.

"I want y'all to sort everything and create some order up there," Miss Hope continued. "I'm putting y'all entirely on your own and trust you to do the job right."

"Yes, Miss Hope," Mandie said.

"Yes, ma'am," Celia agreed.

"Then Uncle Cal will meet y'all up there in the morning. Now, get on with your classes," she said, waving them out the door.

"See you in the morning at ten, Uncle Cal," Mandie said.

The old Negro grinned. "I'll be there, Missy," he replied.

The next morning at the appointed time, Uncle Cal and his wife, Aunt Phoebe, were waiting for the girls.

"Cal, he say fo' me to help Missies, so heah I be," the old servant woman told them.

"Oh, thank you for coming, Aunt Phoebe, but Celia

and I have to do the work," Mandie told her. "I'm glad you came though. I haven't had much chance to see you since Miss Prudence made the rule that we have to get permission to go to your cottage."

"I knows, Missy," Aunt Phoebe said, patting the girl's blonde head. "But I still watches out fo' Missy when she go out in de dahk to see Mistuh Injun Man."

"You do?" Mandie said in surprise. She gave the old woman a hug. "Thanks for watching out for me, Aunt Phoebe."

Uncle Cal jingled something in his pocket. "I'se got de keys," he said, pulling them out and dangling them in front of the girls.

"Uncle Cal, how do you happen to have the keys to everything up here when Miss Hope said all this was mostly stuff the lady left here when she moved?" Mandie said.

"Missy, keys go wid furnichuh. No sense in lady movin' out, leavin' furnichuh and takin' de keys wid huh," he explained.

"You're right. The keys wouldn't be any good without the furniture," Mandie said.

"Lemme see now," Uncle Cal said, trying first one key and then another in the locks of the various pieces of furniture. With some success, he was unlocking wardrobes and chests. Aunt Phoebe walked along behind him, examining the contents of each.

Mandie drew Uncle Cal's attention to the locked trunk on the other side of the attic. "Do you have a key to this trunk, Uncle Cal? This is the trunk that girl, Hilda, was trying to open," Mandie told him.

"I'll sho' see," Uncle Cal replied, making his way over to the big old trunk.

Mandie and Celia watched anxiously as Uncle Cal tried key after key in the lock.

"Missy, don't be no key to fit dat trunk," he told them.

Mandie and Celia both sighed.

"Are you sure?" Mandie asked. "Maybe you missed one. Why don't we go around and leave the key in each lock that it fits and when we run out of keys or locks, we can see what's left," she suggested.

So this they did. But as they finished, there was no leftover key. Every key had been used.

"Were those all the keys Miss Hope had?" Mandie asked.

"Dese all she have in de cab'net. I watches huh git 'em out," the old man assured her.

Aunt Phoebe spoke up. "Dat all de keys, Missy," she said. "Miss Hope done had me goin' all ovuh de house lookin' fo' keys and dey ain't no mo' to be found."

"Do y'all know where this trunk came from?" Mandie asked the old servants.

They both shook their heads.

"Dat trunk done be heah long as I 'membuh," Uncle Cal said.

"I don't nevuh come to de attic," Aunt Phoebe told them, "so I ain't got no idee wheah it come from."

"Maybe the key will turn up somewhere," Mandie said.

Uncle Cal bent to hit the lock with his hand several times, but the lock didn't budge.

"Dat's a good lock. Won't bounce open like some I'se seen," he said.

Mandie's face clouded with disappointment.

"Missy, we'se got all dese othuh things we'se got to straighten out anyhow," Aunt Phoebe said, surveying the room. "That be 'nuff work."

"I know, Aunt Phoebe. Come on, Celia," Mandie said. "You start at that side over there, and I'll start over here in this corner. Let's look through everything real fast and get an idea of what all is here. Then we can decide how to sort things out."

Opening doors and drawers became a time-consuming but interesting chore. The girls held up fancy dresses of bygone days, trying to imagine how they would look in such finery. They modeled ancient hats in front of a mirror on an old vanity. They rummaged through drawers full of quaint trinkets and fancy hair combs. Examining an old wooden box damaged by rats, they found several leather-bound first editions of books long out of print. One drawer of an old chest was crammed full of old yellowed nighties, and a small trunk in the corner contained dozens of pairs of funny-looking ladies' shoes. Everything seemed to be old and worthless.

Suddenly the bell in the back yard rang loudly, bringing the girls back from the old world around them.

"Oh, that's the end of free period!" Celia exclaimed.

"And look how dirty I am," Mandie cried. "Come on, we'll have to hurry." She dropped an old dress she was holding and started for the door. "Good-bye, Uncle Cal and Aunt Phoebe. See y'all later to finish."

"Jes' you be careful flyin' down dem steep steps like dat," Aunt Phoebe called after them.

When the girls reached the bathroom on their floor, they hurriedly washed and then ran to their room to change clothes.

"You might know, that particular key has to be missing," Mandie sighed as she chose a clean dress from the chifferobe.

"Just our luck. All this dirty work and we can't even get that old trunk open," Celia moaned.

Mandie pulled her dress over her head. "We've got to

figure out some way to find that key," she said. "I don't want to do all that dirty work for nothing."

Celia finished buttoning her dress, and the girls grabbed their books from the table to run downstairs.

"Don't give up," Mandie told her friend as they reached the classroom just in time. "Where there's a will there's a way. Somehow we'll find out what's in that trunk."

Chapter 3 / What's in the Trunk?

Miss Hope was watching for Mandie and Celia that evening as the girls gathered around the dining room door for supper. "Amanda, Celia," she said, motioning them aside. "Uncle Cal gave me a good report on your work this morning." She smiled.

"Thank you, Miss Hope," Mandie said.

"But we aren't finished," Celia told her.

"I know. It will undoubtedly take more work to complete the task, but that wasn't why I stopped you. Amanda, your grandmother sent a note over here this afternoon. She was asking permission for your friend, Joe Woodard, and your cat, Snowball—of all things—to visit you." Miss Hope laughed.

"Oh, when, Miss Hope?" Mandie said excitedly.

"Joe will be here at ten o'clock tomorrow morning. He and his father are staying with your grandmother during his school's harvest break," the schoolmistress said. "Now I know that's your free period when you two are supposed to be cleaning the attic, but Miss Prudence forgot about that when she granted permission. So I'll excuse you this one time. The work can be continued the day after tomorrow."

"Oh, thank you, thank you, Miss Hope," Mandie replied.

Miss Hope looked into the dining room. "Get in there quickly now. Miss Prudence is coming in the other door," she said.

As the girls hurried into the dining room, Mandie grasped Celia's hand. "Where there's a will there's a way," she said softly.

"You mean Joe?" Celia asked in a whisper. "To open that trunk?"

"Right." Mandie grinned.

Since no conversation was allowed at the table, the girls had to wait until the meal was over to discuss their plans for the next day. And then they talked well into the night.

Mandie and Celia awoke early the next morning and eagerly dressed for the day. They were impatient throughout breakfast and morning classes. When the bell rang at ten o'clock for free period, Mandie and Celia were the first ones out of the classroom.

"The porch," Mandie called to her friend as she hurried down the hallway.

Celia followed close behind as Mandie pushed open the front screen door. Joe was waiting on the porch swing with Snowball curled up asleep on his knee.

Joe was Mandie's friend from back home in Swain County. A tall, thin, gangly lad with unruly brown hair, quick brown eyes, and a determined chin, Joe towered over tiny Mandie. He was very protective of her, but he also liked to tease her a little.

Mandie ran forward and picked up her kitten, cuddling him to her neck. Snowball woke and began licking his mistress's neck with his little pink tongue. Then perching on her shoulder, he began to purr softly.

"Snowball, I'm so glad to see you," Mandie whispered. "Thanks for bringing Snowball, Joe."

"That's some greeting for a friend you haven't seen for so long," Joe teased, as he stood up.

"You know I'm always glad to see you, Joe," Mandie told him, reaching to take his hand.

"I know, but I always like for you to tell me so," Joe said, squeezing her hand.

Celia watched Mandie and Joe with amusement. "Would y'all like for me to go somewhere and come back later?" she asked.

"Of course not, Celia," Mandie said quickly.

"It's nice to see you again, Celia," Joe said.

Just then Snowball jumped down and landed on the swing. Mandie reached for him.

"Mandie, please don't let him get away," Joe warned. "I'd hate to have to track him down."

Mandie captured the kitten and held him tightly.

"Me, too," Celia added. "Remember when he got loose in this house and we found him with the girl in the attic?"

"Speaking of attics, Joe—" Mandie guided the conversation. "Come on. We want to show you that old trunk in the attic." She turned to enter the house.

"The one Hilda was trying to open?" he asked, following the girls into the hallway inside.

"That's the one," Mandie replied.

The three quietly made their way up to the attic. Mandie, taking the lead, pushed open the door and stood back for Joe and Celia to go inside.

"Wow!" Joe exclaimed, looking around. "Some attic! There's enough furniture up here to furnish ten houses!"

"Not quite," Mandie replied. "There's the trunk over there."

She pointed to the one thing in the attic that remained locked. Celia led the way through the jumbled mess of everything they had opened and started to sort the day before. Mandie stood by the trunk with her arms crossed and a disgusted look on her face.

"You see, it's locked and we can't find a key to fit it," Mandie said, banging the lock with her fist.

"You can't find a key anywhere?" Joe asked.

"No," Celia replied. "Uncle Cal had the keys to everything else, but not to this trunk."

"How are you going to find out what's in it?" Joe asked. Then a grin spread across his face. "I suppose that's what you're planning now," he said. "Always poking and investigating and getting into trouble, both of you."

"I'll have you to know, we have permission to open anything in the attic," Mandie said smugly. "You see, Miss Prudence gave us the job of cleaning this place up—with a little help from Uncle Cal. Now if you could just figure out some way to get this thing open, then we could see what's inside it."

"So that's why you really brought me up here. Well, I'm not a magician. If you don't have a key, there's no way I know to get it open," Joe told her.

"You could break the lock," Celia suggested.

"Break the lock? And get *myself* in trouble?" Joe asked.

"Look! There are Uncle Cal's tools," Mandie said. She bent behind the trunk to pick up a screwdriver and a hammer. "Couldn't you use these to pry it open?"

"Mandie, you're asking for trouble," Joe warned.

"Miss Hope said we could open anything in the attic.

If you're careful and don't damage the trunk, I think it would be all right to force open the lock," Mandie argued. She turned to Celia. "Don't you think it would be all right for us to use these to open it?"

Celia hesitated for a moment and then replied, "I suppose it would be all right. Like Mandie said, Joe, Miss Hope told us we could open anything in the attic."

"Well, then give me those tools," Joe finally agreed. "I'm not even sure these will work. That lock looks all rusted."

"Joe, please hurry," Mandie urged. "We have less than two hours before we have to go to the dining room."

"And my father is coming to get me at twelve o'clock," the boy replied, bending over the trunk with the hammer and screwdriver. The girls hovered near with Snowball perched on Mandie's shoulder. Joe carefully stuck the tip of the screwdriver under the edge of the metal around the keyhole and softly tapped the screwdriver with the hammer. Nothing happened. The strong metal wouldn't yield.

With a sigh, Joe stood up and looked at the trunk and then at the girls.

"Hit it hard," Celia told him.

"What if that metal breaks all up when I hit it real hard? The trunk would be ruined and we'd be in trouble," he reasoned.

"I think it's just stuck with rust," Mandie said. "If we just had something to lubricate it with . . ."

"Just where would you get anything like that?" Joe asked.

"The oil in our lamp!" Mandie said. "Celia, will you go down to our room and get it?"

Celia hurried out of the attic and quickly returned,

holding the oil lamp that usually sat on the table by their bed.

"Here. Let's take the shade off and unscrew this metal thing holding the wick," Mandie told her, taking the lamp apart and giving the pieces to Celia. Then she held up the base with the kerosene in it.

Celia frowned. "Don't use it all up, Mandie, or we won't have any light tonight," Celia warned her.

"If we just pour a little of this on the lock, maybe it will limber up," Mandie said, bending to drip a few drops of the oil on the lock.

At that moment Snowball chose to jump down from Mandie's shoulder. As he did, he hit the lamp base Mandie was holding, and the oil splattered all over the top of the trunk.

Celia snatched a handful of cleaning rags lying nearby and threw one to Joe.

"Quick! Let's clean it off!" she cried, wiping furiously at the oil on the trunk.

Joe helped, but muttered to himself all the while.

"Look!" Mandie exclaimed. "The oil is cleaning the trunk. See how nice it looks where you've rubbed the oil off." Suddenly, bending closer, she gasped. "Why there's a big letter *H* on the lid. Look!"

The three heads bent together to look.

"*H*. That could stand for Hope," Celia suggested.

"Do you suppose this trunk belongs to Miss Hope?" Mandie asked. "But she said the things up here mostly belonged to the lady who lived here before."

"*H* could also stand for Heathwood—or for anything," Joe said. "There's no telling what's in this trunk, Mandie, or who it belonged to."

"Miss Hope said we could open anything," Celia reminded them. "If there was something she didn't want us to open, she would have said so."

"Right," Mandie agreed. "Try it again, Joe."

"If you say so," Joe muttered, his thin face giving them an exasperated look.

The girls watched anxiously as Joe picked up the tools and began tapping the screwdriver harder to force the lock. Snowball roamed through the attic.

"Uncle Cal hit it real hard when he tried to knock it open, like this," Mandie said, hitting the lock with her hand.

"That won't work," Joe said.

"Maybe this will," Mandie suggested. She climbed upon the top of the trunk and stood there. "You stick the screwdriver under the lock and hit it with the hammer. At the same time I'll jump up and stomp down hard on the lid."

"Mandie, please be careful," the boy told her, bending to do as she said. "Here we go—one, two, three, jump!"

The first time they were not together for their assault on the trunk.

Snowball quickly moved away from the noise and stood watching. The second time Joe and Mandie succeeded. The old lock flipped loose from the bottom plate in the trunk lid, and the three of them cheered and laughed.

"It worked!" Mandie cried, jumping down from the trunk. "Help me get the lid up. Those hooks there are holding it."

Celia and Joe released the hooks, and Mandie pushed the heavy lid up. Snowball immediately jumped up on the edge of the opened trunk. As he looked inside he hissed and hunched his back.

The three young people gasped in horror as they stared into the opened trunk.

Celia jumped back.

"What is it?" she cried.

"They're animals or something—all furry!" Mandie cringed.

Joe bent down for a closer look. "If they're animals, they're all dead," he said. Reaching for an old poker which stood against the wall, he poked the contents of the trunk.

"Joe, what are you doing?" Celia cried.

Joe reached into the trunk and began pulling out long pieces of fur. Swinging them in the air, he laughed. "Look! Just old furs!" he declared.

The two girls drew closer to inspect what he had in his hands. Snowball ducked out of the way of the swinging furs and huddled against Mandie's ankles.

"You're right!" Mandie laughed. "They're someone's old furs. And here are some fur hats."

When she pulled the hats out of the trunk, something caught her eye. "There's something metal down under here," she said, digging beneath the furs.

Celia and Joe helped empty the trunk, throwing the furs and hats onto the floor. Finally Joe pulled out an old metal candy box and handed it to Mandie.

"All tied up with pink ribbons!" Mandie exclaimed. She pulled the faded ribbons from around the box labeled *Baker's Chocolates,* and lifted the lid, revealing stacks of old letters.

"Oh, look!" Mandie said, sitting down on the floor to empty the contents of the box. Joe and Celia sat down beside her while Snowball nosed through the pile of papers.

"Let's see whose letters these are," Mandie said.

Celia shuffled the envelopes. "There's no name on any that I can see," she replied. "They're all addressed to 'My One and Only Love.' That's all that's on the envelopes."

"Well, let's look inside," Mandie urged.

Each of the young people opened one of the envelopes. The letter paper had turned to a brownish hue and the handwriting was barely readable.

Joe looked up from the letter he held in his hand. "This one is addressed to 'My One and Only Love,' and it's signed 'Your Truelove,' " he said. "How mushy!"

"So is this one!" Mandie told him.

"And this one, too," Celia added.

"Maybe if we read them we could tell who they belong to," said Mandie.

Joe objected. "Mandie, these are someone's personal property," he said. "You wouldn't want someone reading your private letters, would you?"

"Oh, Joe, these are so old that whoever wrote them is ancient by now," Mandie argued. "They may not even be alive. I don't see any year on any of them, just the month and the day, but the paper is so old it's crumbling around the edges." Mandie returned to reading the letter in her hand.

"Miss Hope said we could open anything in the attic," Celia reminded him again. "Besides, if we fold these up and put them back in the box, who will ever know we read them? We just won't talk about it to anyone."

Mandie looked up. "Listen to this," she said, beginning to read. " 'I waited in vain until midnight last night in the cabin in the woods where we always meet, my love. My poor heart cried for you so loudly, I shouldn't be surprised if your dear heart heard its cry. I know you cannot always manage to keep our tryst—' "

"Mandie!" Joe interrupted. "What do you want to read all that sickening rigamarole for?"

"If these two people met in a cabin in the woods, it must have been a forbidden love affair," Mandie reasoned. "I wonder where the cabin in the woods is."

Celia gasped. "This one says 'the place where the diamonds are hidden must be changed.' "

"Diamonds!" Joe repeated. "Let me see what you're reading."

Celia handed him the letter, indicating the paragraph. Joe quickly scanned the page.

"Well, if there are diamonds hidden somewhere, I say let's find them!" Joe exclaimed.

Mandie sighed with relief. They had won Joe over. She moved closer to look at the letter he was holding.

"But there isn't any kind of a clue about where to look," Mandie said.

"We haven't read all of them yet," Celia reminded her. "Maybe we can find something in another letter." She reached for another envelope and slipped out the folded sheets of paper.

"We'd better hurry," Mandie warned. "I'm sure the bell's going to ring soon."

The three hastily read the letters, stuffing each one back into its envelope when they were finished. Snowball played nearby with the ribbon from the box.

"This one mentions a 'dangerous enemy.' " Mandie said. "This is some mystery."

Joe looked up from the letter in his hand. "Whoever this person was writing to must have been adopted," he said. "This one says, 'I am sure your real mother and father would have approved of our courtship. Your adopted parents treat you as though you were twelve years old instead of seventeen,' " he read. "Well, now we know that the person who received these letters was seventeen years old and had two sets of parents."

"Here's more in this letter," Celia said. "This says, 'I pray to God every day that we will be allowed to marry. We must have faith, my love, and trust in Him to lead us and guide us in the right pathway.' " Celia put down the letter. "Oh, how sad! Two people in love who are not allowed to marry."

"Here's that 'dangerous enemy' again," said Mandie. "It says, 'We must be ever watchful for my dangerous enemy. He could cause us great heartache if he learned of our secret meetings, my love. He is so desperately in love with you, and he knows that you scorn his attention. I am afraid to imagine what he might do if he found out about us, especially since he knows your parents favor him to be your husband.' " Mandie's eyes widened. "Listen. It gets even better."

Dramatically, she read on. " 'It fills my heart with great satisfaction to know that his lips have never touched yours, his hands have never held yours. My heart is humble, my love, to know that you prefer my lowly existence over his wealth and power. My heart is forever yours. For the rest of this world and on into the next, I am forever Your Truelove.' " Mandie sighed. "Oh, if I only knew who wrote these letters! This is all so mysterious. No names are mentioned anywhere."

Just then, the bell in the backyard clanged. The two girls jumped up and quickly began to stuff the letters back into the envelopes, returning them to the box.

"But we didn't get to read all of them," Joe protested, helping the girls with the letters.

"I know," Mandie said with disappointment. "But Miss Hope said you'd be in town while your school is out. Can you come back tomorrow?" she asked. "It would have to be during our afternoon free period because we have to work in the attic in the morning."

"Could you and Celia come to your Grandmother's tonight for supper?" Joe asked.

"And bring the letters with us?" Celia suggested.

"Sure," Mandie agreed. "Just tell Grandmother we'd like to come. She'll have to send a note to Miss Hope."

"Just don't forget the letters," Joe said picking up Snowball, as they prepared to leave the attic.

Mandie hugged the candy box to herself. "We'll take these down to our room right now," she said, quickly leading the way down the stairs. At the landing to the third floor Mandie and Celia said good-bye to Joe and Snowball, then ran into their room to hide the candy box in Mandie's traveling bag.

"I won't be able to concentrate on a thing today until I get a chance to read the rest of those letters," Mandie told Celia as they hurried on down to the dining room for the noon meal.

"Me either," Celia agreed. "This might turn out to be exciting."

"And if that dangerous enemy is still around, it could be dangerous," Mandie reminded her with a laugh.

"But no one knows we've found the letters," Celia said. No one knew then, but someone would find out later.

Chapter 4 / Secret Plans

As they sat around her grandmother's supper table that night, Mandie was glad for a chance to talk to Joe's father. "How is Hilda, Dr. Woodard? Have you seen her since you came to Asheville?"

"Why, yes, Amanda. As a matter of fact, I have," the doctor replied. "She's healthier and more alert now, but she still won't talk to anyone. We aren't even sure if she *can* talk. But she seems as happy as a dead pig in the sunshine."

Joe looked at his father with pride. "My father knows the doctors at the sanitarium," he said, "and he really keeps track of how Hilda is doing."

"I'm glad you were able to find some help for her. Thank you for all you've done, Doctor Woodard," Mandie said. "I think about Hilda once in a while, and I wonder if she would know Celia and me if she saw us."

"There's only one way to answer that, Amanda. We'll just have to take you girls to visit her." He glanced across the table at Mrs. Taft. "If it's all right with your grandmother," he said.

Celia looked worried. "What about Miss Hope? Do you think she'll allow us to go?"

Mrs. Taft smiled. "I'll send her word that you two girls will be accompanying Dr. Woodard to visit Hilda as soon as he lets me know when," she said.

"Thank you, Grandmother," Mandie said.

"That would be wonderful, Mrs. Taft. Thank you," Celia echoed.

Mandie changed the subject. "How is the work going on the hospital for the Cherokees, Dr. Woodard?" she asked.

Celia looked puzzled. "What hospital?"

Dr. Woodard laughed. "Why, Celia, I'm surprised Amanda hasn't told you about that." He laughed again. "Your friend is quite a heroine among the Cherokees. She and her friends found a great deal of gold which belonged to the Indians, and they let *her* decide what to do with it."

"Oh, I remember now," Celia replied, "but go on. I like to hear about all Mandie's adventures."

Joe took the plate of chocolate cake the maid offered him and continued the story. "There's not much more to tell. Mandie decided the Cherokees needed a hospital, and it's being built right now!" he explained.

"I think that's wonderful!" Celia looked at her friend with admiration.

Mandie blushed slightly, trying to ignore the praise. "Then the building is going all right?" she asked Dr. Woodard.

"No hitches at all," Dr. Woodard assured her. "Everything is right on schedule. Maybe some day soon you can come and see for yourself what it looks like."

"Could I, Grandmother?" Mandie asked excitedly.

"You know that is up to your mother, Amanda," Mrs. Taft replied. "I'm sorry, dear, but I can't let you go without her permission."

"Why don't you write and ask your mother about it?" Dr. Woodard suggested. "Then we could make arrangements for me to come and get you."

"I will, Dr. Woodard. I think maybe mother will let me go," Mandie replied.

When they had all finished their cake, Mrs. Taft called the maid to clear the table. "You young people may go on into the sitting room while Dr. Woodard and I stay here for our coffee," she said. "Just remember you must be back to school before the ten o'clock bell rings tonight," she reminded the girls.

Mandie, Celia, and Joe hurried out of the dining room and down the hallway to the sitting room where Snowball waited for them.

"Did you bring the letters?" Joe asked.

"Oh, yes," Mandie replied, finding her school bag in a corner by Celia's. "The candy box is under my books. Here."

She handed the *Baker's Chocolates* box to Joe, and they all sat on the carpet to read the "epistles of love," as Celia had begun to call them. Each of them took a letter and began to read silently. Snowball curled up on Mandie's lap and began to purr.

"I keep finding that 'dangerous enemy' in the letters I read," remarked Mandie, returning a letter to its envelope.

"Here it is again about the diamonds." Celia began to read aloud. " 'The diamonds are not safe. I believe someone saw me last night when I checked to see that they were still there. We're going to have to find another hiding place for them, my love.' " Celia looked up. "I wish whoever wrote these letters had been a little clearer about these diamonds."

"So do I," Joe agreed. "I have an idea this dangerous enemy must have been the one who saw him check on the diamonds. He was probably spying on them all the time."

"I think so, too," Mandie agreed, trying to keep Snowball from pawing the letter she was unfolding. "Snowball, behave yourself or I'll make you get down," she scolded.

"Do you really think that someone was spying on them?" Celia asked.

"If we can get finished reading all of these letters, maybe we'll find out," Joe said. "They seem to be in order by the month. If we read in that sequence I think we'll understand more."

"We'd better hurry," Celia said.

"Yes, we agreed that we wouldn't tell anyone about this, so that means that if my grandmother and Joe's father come in here, we'll have to hide these letters," Mandie warned.

Joe opened another envelope. "This is only one page," he said. "It just says, 'Please make every effort possible to meet me tonight at the cabin in the woods, my love. My eyes haven't feasted on you for three days now. I can't eat or sleep until I see for myself that you are all right. I will be waiting, and I pray that God will show you a way to meet me.' " Joe gave a low whistle. "That's some flowery language," he said.

Mandie looked up suddenly. "Something just dawned on me," she said. "There's no mention in any of these letters so far that the person who received them ever answered back."

"Come to think of it, you're right," Joe replied. "There isn't anything about receiving an answer." He thought for a moment. "But maybe this person had no way of send-ing him an answer. Maybe she couldn't write to him with-out running the risk of her parents finding out."

"Then how did she manage to receive these letters without their knowledge?" Celia asked.

"I'm wondering why the girl's parents didn't want her to see this man," Mandie said. "What reason could they have had? What could have been wrong with him?"

"He was poor, Mandie, remember?" Joe reminded her. "There was a letter that mentioned his lowly existence and the other man's power and wealth."

"Why should that make a difference?" Mandie asked, stroking her kitten.

"Oh, Mandie, I keep forgetting you were brought up in a log cabin way back there in Swain County, and you never mingled with the big world," Joe said. "Now please don't take that the wrong way. That's what I admire about you—"

Mandie jumped up, knocking Snowball to the floor. "Joe Woodard, I'll have you to know that you were also brought up back there in Swain County. And just tell me what's wrong with that?" Her blue eyes flashed in anger. "I think these city people are all a great put-on with their silly social graces. They're not honest with themselves or with the world. They're always pretending. At least I was always taught to speak the truth, whether it hurts or not."

Joe caught Mandie's hand in his as she waved it through the air. "Now hold on a minute, Mandie," he begged her. "I just said that's what I admire about you— your honesty and outspokenness. People always know where they stand with you. But you must remember, these city people, as you call them, have always had some strange ideas about marrying their daughters off. Society people have always hunted for a rich man to be their son-in-law—someone they thought would be able financially to take care of their precious daughter." Joe waved one of the letters in front of her. "Evidently this man was not rich or in high society. Therefore, the girl's parents thought he was not good enough for their daughter, no matter how much the two loved each other. Money came first, and if they were fortunate, the money had love attached to it. Don't you understand?"

Mandie plopped back down on the floor and picked up Snowball. "I know what you mean. I just don't see how people can live like that. I don't think God meant it to be that way."

Joe scooted closer to her and again took her small hand in his. "Mandie, I told you a long time ago that I wanted to marry you when we grow up—long before either of us knew that you would inherit your Uncle John's wealth someday," he reminded her. "Everyone knew your uncle was already the richest man this side of Richmond, but when he married your mother with all her money, that probably made them the wealthiest couple in the whole southeast. But we didn't even know about any money when your father died and left you with that terrible stepmother." He patted her hand. "I told you then I would take care of you, and I still plan to if you haven't changed your mind," he promised.

Celia sat quietly, pretending to read more of the letters while Mandie and Joe talked things out.

"Oh, phooey on all that money, anyway. I don't want any of it," Mandie insisted. "I just want my father's farm back from that woman he married, and when he died you promised me you would get it back for me."

"And I intend to keep my promise, Mandie," Joe told

her. "It may take a few years, but I promise you I will get your father's property back for you."

Finally Celia shook her head. "Hey, come on. Draw the curtain. We'd better hurry and get these read."

Mandie and Joe smiled at each other and then laughed, returning to their task of reading the faded letters.

"Money again," Mandie fussed as she read on. "I wish I could have talked to this girl's parents to make them understand that love is much, much more important than all the money in the world."

The three young people finished reading the rest of the letters and sat back to discuss them.

"We have to make some plans to solve this mystery—that's for sure," Mandie told the others. "We'll probably be finished with the attic tomorrow, and then we'll have our free period free again." She thought for a moment. "I think we should begin by asking Miss Hope a few questions," she said.

"Like what?" Joe asked.

Mandie stared into space. "Like whether she was adopted or—"

"You don't think Miss Hope was the one who received these letters, do you?" Celia interrupted.

"You never can tell. You have to eliminate a lot of possibilities in order to find the right answer," Mandie replied. "Even though she's old now, Miss Hope is still pretty. Some man could have been hopelessly in love with her."

"What are you going to ask her?" Joe probed. "Are you going to tell her you've been reading some love letters that may have belonged to her?"

"Of course not," Mandie replied. "We won't let anyone

know we found these letters. But we could find out if she was adopted. And we could also ask her about the woman who owned this house before. Maybe the letters were written to her."

"Sure, Mandie, I can just see a married woman with a daughter keeping her old love letters in the attic," Joe teased.

"Joe, you have no imagination at all," Mandie said. "Just remember they were locked up in a trunk with no key to be found. But on the other hand . . ." She paused to think. ". . . if the letters belong to Miss Hope, the trunk would have been moved here from her parents' home, wherever that was."

"In that case we'll never find the cabin in the woods the man wrote about," Joe reminded her. "It would have been near some other house."

"I think we ought to search near here for the cabin," Celia told them. "There are woods beyond the flower gardens, and we've never been down there. We don't know for sure it *wasn't* near the school."

"You're right," Joe agreed. "If we can find the cabin we'll know the girl lived in this house."

"Well, not exactly," Mandie said. "We might just find any old cabin in those woods. We won't know for sure that it was the one where they met."

"But like you said, we have to eliminate some possibilities to solve anything," Joe reminded her.

"All right. Celia and I will question Miss Hope," Mandie resolved. "Joe, can you come back to our school tomorrow afternoon? We have a free period from three-thirty until suppertime."

"Sure," Joe replied, his eyes twinkling. "I'd sure like to know more about those diamonds."

"When are we going to visit Hilda?" Celia asked.

"Let's do that Saturday," Mandie suggested. "We'll have more free time then anyway. Is that all right?"

Joe nodded.

"It's fine with me," Celia said. "Mandie, don't forget to ask your grandmother to send Miss Hope a note. You know how strict they are about visitors, and we don't want to break any more rules, remember?"

"I'll ask Grandmother to tell Miss Hope that Joe will be coming to visit us in the afternoon," Mandie promised. "She knows Joe and Dr. Woodard, so I don't think she'll mind." Mandie squeezed Joe's hand. "We'll have plenty of time to explore the woods."

"We sure don't want to get into any more trouble," Celia repeated.

As the three young people made their plans, they had no idea what kind of trouble lay ahead.

Chapter 5 / Search in the Woods

By the time their free period was over next morning, Mandie and Celia had the attic in neat order with the help of Uncle Cal and Aunt Phoebe. The four of them stood back to admire their work.

Mandie glanced around at the old furniture lined up along the wall. Worn trunks and discolored boxes were neatly spaced nearby. "I think we did a pretty good job," she said.

"Me, too," Celia agreed.

"Dis place ain't nevuh been dis clean," Uncle Cal remarked.

Aunt Phoebe gave both girls a squeeze. "Both my lil' Missies make good housekeepuhs someday," she said.

"That wasn't such a big job," Celia said.

"No, but that's because we had Uncle Cal and Aunt Pheobe to help us," Mandie replied. "Without them we would have been working here for days. Well, I guess we'd better get cleaned up before the bell rings to go to the dining room. Thanks for your help, Aunt Phoebe and Uncle Cal," she said, giving them both a hug.

"Lawsy mercy, Missy, dat's whut de good Lawd put

us all heah fo', to help one 'nuthuh," Aunt Phoebe said. "Now you gits goin' 'fo' you bees late."

"You Missies don't wanta git in no mo' trouble," Uncle Cal warned. "Miz Hope mought not 'llow de doctuh's son come visit."

As they started down the steps, Mandie turned to the old Negro. "You're going after Joe at three-thirty, aren't you, Uncle Cal?"

"Yessum, Missy. I'se gwine to brang him heah. Miz Hope done tol' me to go," the old man confirmed. "But, Missy, please be careful and don' make no mo' trouble."

"I'm trying real hard, Uncle Cal," Mandie told him. "Uncle Cal, and Aunt Phoebe, have y'all been working here ever since Miss Prudence and Miss Hope opened this school? Did you know the lady who owned this house before they did?"

Aunt Phoebe shook her head, and Uncle Cal replied, "No, Missy. Phoebe and me had jes' got hitched 'bout de time dis school opened up. We lived on a farm. Jes' come heah 'bout twenty yeahs ago. But my—"

The bell in the backyard interrupted their conversation, and the girls turned to run down the stairs.

"See you later," Mandie called back to them.

"Thanks," Celia said, quickly following her friend.

Stopping by the bathroom, the girls hastily cleaned up, then ran to their room to take off their aprons and smooth their hair before hurrying down to the dining room.

"I guess that means we won't get any clues from Aunt Phoebe and Uncle Cal," Mandie told Celia as they walked briskly down the hallway. "They wouldn't know anything about our mystery if they didn't live here back then."

The day seemed to drag as the girls waited impatiently for three-thirty. When Joe arrived, they would explore the woods. The girls' minds were not on their lessons.

April Snow, the tall, dark-haired troublemaker at the girls' school, bent across the aisle and whispered to Mandie. "What kind of trouble are y'all thinking up this time?" she asked.

Mandie felt the blood rush to her face and tried to ignore the girl. April was always trying to start something. Mandie did her best to control her temper.

Even though the girl had called Mandie a half-breed savage one day, creating a stir that resulted in both of them being suspended from school, Mandie had tried to forgive and forget. But somehow she just couldn't be friends with April. And April took every opportunity to make verbal jabs at her.

Mandie fidgeted nervously, silently asking God to help her remain calm. She drew in a deep breath and blew it out.

Miss Cameron paused in her recitation about the battle of Cowpens in the Revolutionary War and looked at Mandie with concern. "Amanda, are you all right?" she asked.

"Yes, ma'am, Miss Cameron. I'm fine," Mandie replied quickly. Sitting up straight in her chair, she tried to focus her attention on the lesson.

"Now, young ladies, as I was saying." Miss Cameron continued with the events that led to the victory at Cowpens.

When at last three-thirty came, Mandie and Celia raced upstairs to leave their books, then hurried back downstairs.

"Well, here I am," Joe said as he met them at the

front door. "I didn't bring Snowball."

"That's good. He might get lost. We're all ready to go," Mandie replied. "Let's go outside."

The three young people walked out into the yard beneath the giant magnolia trees.

Joe eyed the girls suspiciously. "Are y'all sure you want to go down there into the woods with those fine dresses on?" he asked.

"Fine? These are just our everyday school dresses," Mandie told him.

"I remember when that would have been finer than your Sunday-go-to-meeting clothes back in Swain County," he said with a laugh. "Well then, what are we waiting for?" As he turned to hurry down the hillside, the girls followed close behind but paused when they reached the edge of the thick woods.

"Looks like an awful lot of underbrush," Joe commented.

"Just a minute," Mandie said. Running toward a huge tree nearby, she brought out a hoe and axe from behind it. "Here! Celia and I borrowed these from the tool shed. We figured we might have to chop a path to get through," she said. "Joe, you take the axe and Celia and I will use the hoe."

Joe threw the axe across his thin shoulder and led the way into the trees. Mandie followed, using the hoe handle like a walking stick, and Celia brought up the rear. Briars caught in their clothes, tree limbs swept their heads, and unseen rocks in the undergrowth bruised the girls' feet through the thin soles of their dress shoes, but they didn't complain.

Joe stopped for a moment after traipsing through the dense forest for what seemed like hours. "Suppose we get lost?" he asked.

"Impossible," Mandie told him. "Remember, I'm part Cherokee. I've watched my Cherokee kinpeople mark a trail."

"Is that why you've been breaking twigs on bushes all along the way?" Celia asked.

"That's the way you do it," Mandie explained.

"All right, my papoose. Please mark a good trail so we can find the way back," Joe teased her.

"Will do, my brave. You keep a lookout for panthers," Mandie replied, going along with his joking.

The farther they went into the woods, the darker it became. None of them had a watch, so they didn't know what time it was.

But finally Joe stopped again. "I think we'd better go back," he said. "It seems to be getting late."

Mandie sighed. "I wish we could have found something," she said.

"Couldn't we come back later?" Celia asked.

"Later?" Mandie frowned. "You mean after dark?"

"Isn't it the night for Uncle Ned to come visit you? The moon changes tonight," Celia observed.

"He's supposed to come tonight, but he doesn't come until after ten o'clock. That will be entirely too late," Mandie told her. "On the other hand, how about tomorrow? I could ask Uncle Ned to come back tomorrow afternoon and go with us. He would know how to get around in a place like this better than we do."

"That's a good idea," Joe agreed.

"I'll ask him when he comes tonight," Mandie promised.

The three found their way back through the woods and left the tools at the hiding place. As they hurried up the hillside, they saw Uncle Cal waiting with the rig to take Joe back to Mandie's grandmother's house.

"Hurry, Missies. 'Bout late fo' suppuh," the old black man warned as they came up the driveway. "Come on, doctuh's son. Let's go."

The girls ran for the front door.

"See you tomorrow," Joe called to them as he stepped into the rig.

Mandie and Celia hurried down the hallway and joined the line of students as they began filing into the dining room for the first seating of the evening meal. Miss Prudence glanced sharply at them, and the girls suddenly realized that they must look quite disheveled after their trek through the woods. But it was too late to do anything about it.

Mandie patted her hair and whispered to Celia. "We might be in trouble," she said, holding up crossed fingers.

Celia straightened her skirt. "I sure hope not," she replied.

The meal went swiftly, and the girls were dismissed as the second group of students waited outside the doorway. Steering clear of Miss Prudence, Mandie and Celia hurried upstairs.

Standing in front of the long mirror in their room, the two girls could now see why Miss Prudence had given them such a sharp look. Celia had a faint scratch across her cheek. Mandie's chin was smudged. Both girls' hair looked as though it hadn't been combed for weeks.

Shocked at her appearance, Mandie fell across the bed laughing, and Celia joined her.

"How terrible we look and none of the girls at the table seemed to notice," Mandie said between giggles. "Not a single person even smiled at us."

"Miss Prudence noticed," Celia said, sitting up. "I wonder if we'll be called in for it."

Mandie groaned. "I hope not," she said. "But right now I think we'd better get cleaned up a little and make a ladylike appearance on the veranda with the others."

"Right," Celia agreed.

Suddenly Mandie whirled around. "Celia, I forgot," she said. "We haven't told Miss Hope that we're finished with the attic."

"That's right," Celia replied.

"Let's find her tonight and tell her, so she won't expect us up there tomorrow," Mandie suggested. "She ought to be finished with her supper by the time we get ourselves presentable."

Not satisfied with their dirty, rumpled clothes, the girls changed dresses and carefully combed their hair. By the time they left their room, the only remaining trace of their trip into the woods was the scratch on Celia's cheek, which she tried to cover with bath powder.

Downstairs they found Miss Hope just as she was going into her office.

Mandie stopped her at the door. "Miss Hope, we're all done in the attic," she said. "Everything is clean and orderly."

"That's nice," Miss Hope replied. "Come on into my office a minute. I'd like to talk to you girls."

Mandie's heart beat wildly; they were in trouble again! Celia turned to look at Mandie as they followed Miss Hope into her office.

Miss Hope sat down behind her desk, her face giving no indication of her mood. "Sit down. This will only take but a minute," she said.

The girls sat gingerly on the edges of their chairs, waiting for their scolding.

"Amanda, I know Dr. Woodard's son plans to call on you every afternoon this week," Miss Hope began, "but I thought you girls might like to go to the farm with me tomorrow afternoon. As you probably know, the school owns its own farm, which is just a few miles from here. We usually take all the girls from the school out there two or three times during the semester for candy pullings and hayrides, and there's a nice lake which freezes over for ice skating in the winter," Miss Hope told them. "I have to go out there tomorrow to check over the books. Since you girls have done such a good job of mending your ways, I thought it would be a little treat for you to go along."

"Tomorrow afternoon?" Mandie asked slowly. They had planned another search for the cabin the next afternoon.

"Yes, I have to go tomorrow," the schoolmistress explained. "Miss Prudence and I can't both leave the school at the same time, and I don't like going alone, so I thought I'd ask you two."

Celia looked at Mandie, then at Miss Hope. "I would love to go with you, Miss Hope," she said. "Mandie can stay here and visit with Joe. She doesn't get to see him very often."

"Neither one of you has to go," Miss Hope told them. "I can ask one of the other girls."

"I'd like to see the farm," Celia said. "Really and truly. I know you have horses out there, and I've missed mine at home so much since I've been here."

Mandie leaned forward. "I would like to go, too, Miss Hope, but since Joe is only going to be in town during his school break, could I please wait and go next time?" she asked.

"Of course, Amanda," Miss Hope replied. "Now, Celia, meet me here at two o'clock tomorrow afternoon. I'll have you excused from your classes then. And please wear something rough if you plan to explore the farm."

"Thank you, Miss Hope," Celia promised. "I'll be here at two o'clock."

The girls left the office and went out onto the veranda.

Celia explained to her friend. "Miss Hope has been so nice to us, Mandie, I just couldn't let her down," she said. "I knew you didn't want to go. But now you, and Joe, and Uncle Ned can look for the cabin, and I'll go to the farm."

"Thanks so much, Celia," Mandie replied. "Miss Hope didn't say when you'd return, but I imagine you'll be back in time for supper. I'll tell you if we found anything then." Mandie blew out her breath. "Thank goodness that was all she wanted with us," she said.

That night, when Uncle Ned came, Mandie tried to explain to him about the letters in the trunk. "You see, the letters don't have any names on them, and not even the year. They look so old and crumbly," she said.

"Papoose, letters belong to someone. Papoose not get into business of other people. Other people be hurt if know Papoose find letters and read," the old Indian cautioned her.

"We're not going to let anybody know about them," Mandie said. "We haven't told anyone but you—not even my grandmother or Joe's father. We'd just like to solve the mystery. So will you come back tomorrow afternoon and go with Joe and me into the woods to look for that cabin mentioned in the letters?" she begged. "Please, Uncle Ned."

"I come," the old man said as he stood up. "I promise

Jim Shaw I watch over Papoose. So I watch over Papoose in woods tomorrow. I wait by great trees in forest for Papoose and Doctor Son."

"Thank you, Uncle Ned. Thank you." Mandie rose to kiss the old man's withered cheek.

"I go now. Papoose go back to big house," he told her.

Mandie ran across the grass in the moonlight, then turned to wave as she entered the back door of the house. Although she couldn't see him, she knew her Indian friend would wait in the shadows until she was safely inside.

Mandie hurried into the kitchen and pushed the bolt across the back door. Suddenly she heard faint footsteps coming down the servants' stairs. Ducking inside the huge pantry, she pulled the door almost shut and held her breath. Her heart pounded loudly.

She listened in fear as the footsteps continued across the kitchen floor. Then there was the click of the bolt as the door softly opened and closed. Whoever it was had gone outside.

Mandie raced up the stairs in the dark, rushed into her room, and ran to the window to look down into the yard. There was April Snow walking across the lawn, and she sat down on the very bench where Mandie had just been with Uncle Ned.

"That was a close call!" Mandie exclaimed in a whisper.

Celia rushed over to see what Mandie was looking at below. "She didn't see you, did she?" Celia whispered back.

"No, thank goodness," Mandie replied softly, explaining what had happened. "She was about one minute too late."

Since their window was open, both girls spoke quietly, knowing their voices might carry in the stillness of the night.

"I'd like to know what she's doing out there at this time of the night," Mandie whispered.

"She's probably spying on you," Celia said. "Remember that night she locked us out, and Aunt Phoebe had to use her key to let us back in? April knows you go out sometimes late at night, but she hasn't found out why yet."

"I sure hope she never figures it out," Mandie replied.

Chapter 6 / Cabin Ruins

The next morning Mandie and Celia encountered Miss Hope in the hallway.

Smiling, the schoolmistress smoothed a stray lock of hair into place. "Celia, we'll have another girl with us this afternoon when we go to the farm," she said. "April Snow has asked permission to go."

Celia and Mandie silently exchanged glances.

"Is something wrong, dears?" the woman asked.

"Oh, no, ma'am. We're fine," Mandie replied. "We were just sort of surprised that April wants to go out into the country."

"Surprised?" Miss Hope asked.

Celia fidgeted with the sash on her dress. "You know, we figured she was strictly a city girl," she said.

"Well, yes, I thought so too. But when she heard me telling Uncle Cal to get the rig ready at two o'clock for Celia and me to go to the farm, she asked to go along," Miss Hope explained. "Excuse me now. I must hurry. I have to teach this next class. I'll see you at two, Celia."

"Yes, ma'am," Celia answered as Miss Hope hurried down the hallway.

"This spells t-r-o-u-b-l-e," Mandie said as they went up the stairs to their room.

"I think you're right," Celia agreed.

The two girls plopped down across the bed in their room and began to discuss the situation.

"I think we ought to talk to Miss Hope as soon as possible and try to find out whether she or Miss Prudence could have been adopted. They don't look at all alike," Mandie reasoned. "Miss Prudence is so tall and dark. And Miss Hope is so short and fair."

"Well, maybe." Celia didn't seem convinced. "They certainly don't look like sisters, but then there are some sisters who don't favor each other at all."

"We also need to ask her the name of the lady they bought this house from," Mandie said. "I was hoping you'd have a chance on the way to the farm, but since April Snow is going, we'll have to wait."

"Maybe we could talk to her after supper tonight," Celia suggested.

"We can try," Mandie said. "I do hope Joe and Uncle Ned and I can find the cabin in the woods today."

At three-thirty that afternoon, Mrs. Taft sent Joe over in her buggy with his promise to be ready and waiting at five o'clock when she sent the buggy back for him.

Celia had left with Miss Hope and April Snow at two o'clock as arranged. Mandie waited for Joe in the alcove near the front door.

As soon as she saw her grandmother's buggy approach, Mandie ran outside. "I'm ready, Joe," she told the boy as he stepped down and handed Mandie her white kitten. "Celia had to go to the school's farm with Miss Hope, but Uncle Ned said he would wait for us at the edge of the trees." She rubbed Snowball's soft fur and put him on her shoulder.

"I'll be ready at five o'clock," Joe called back to Ben, the Negro driver of Mrs. Taft's rig.

Joe scooped up Snowball, caught Mandie's hand, and together they hurried down to the edge of the woods. They stopped there to watch for Uncle Ned. Mandie knew the old Indian would not come out of hiding until he knew they were there and no one else was around. Sure enough, he stepped forward from behind the huge tree where they had hidden the tools.

"We make haste," the old Indian greeted them. "Papoose not be late back to supper."

Mandie ran forward and took his wrinkled, weathered hand. "Did you find the hoe and the axe, Uncle Ned?" she asked.

"I find," Uncle Ned replied.

The three of them walked the short distance to the tree where the tools were hidden. Uncle Ned took the axe and handed the hoe to Joe. Then he silently led the way into the woods.

After they had scrambled through the weeds and underbrush for several mintues, Uncle Ned left the path they had chopped out the day before. He veered to the right into the heart of the forest.

"Cabin not on trail," he told them. "I look while wait. Cabin must be by water. Water this way."

They tromped on.

After a while, they heard the sound of running water in the distance, and the old Indian led them straight to it. The peaceful, rippling brook, surrounded by lush, green foliage, invited them to rest a while, but Uncle Ned pressed on, following the creek bank uphill. The birds singing in the trees fluttered away as the intruders passed by.

Suddenly, there was a crash in the bushes. The three froze as a beautiful doe bounded into view. Then the frightened animal turned and ran back into the underbrush. Snowball saw the doe and tried to get down from Mandie's shoulder.

"Snowball, be still. You're not getting down to chase that poor doe," Mandie scolded as they walked on. "Besides, you'd better pick on something your own size." She held him tightly as he squirmed on her shoulder.

Uncle Ned stopped in front of them and seemed to be listening to something in the woods.

"What is it, Uncle Ned?" Mandie whispered.

"Sound. I hear sound," he muttered, stealthily moving forward.

The two young people quietly followed Uncle Ned to the edge of a wide clearing in the middle of the trees, where the creek wound along to one side. Uncle Ned raised his hand, and the young people stopped behind some trees. They stood and listened. There was a sound of clinking metal nearby. It seemed to come from the far side of the clearing. The old Indian moved around the clearing, staying behind the trees. The young people followed noiselessly.

When they reached the other side of the clearing, they came upon some old timbers lying on the ground. A stone chimney stood tall and lonely just inside the cluster of trees near the creek.

Mandie gasped. "The cabin!" she exclaimed.

A loud scurrying noise startled them for a moment. Then they saw two squirrels fleeing from the fallen timber. Snowball broke loose from Mandie's grasp and jumped down to chase the squirrels.

"Snowball! Come back here!" Mandie demanded.

The kitten stopped at the fallen timber and sniffled around. Mandie dashed forward to grab him. As she picked him up, she noticed a piece of an old chain tangled in the logs. Evidently the squirrels had been shaking it as they nosed into the rubble.

Mandie lifted the end of the chain and rattled it to show Joe and Uncle Ned. "Here's the noise." She laughed.

"Cabin been here," the old Indian stated, stooping to look at its remains.

Mandie grinned at Joe. "I think we've found the cabin in the woods—or what's left of it—don't you?"

"Maybe," Joe said. "It must have been awfully old to be all fallen down and rotted like this."

Uncle Ned straightened up from his inspection of the timbers. He pointed to the ground. "Burn," he said. "Cabin burn."

Mandie and Joe bent to look. Beneath the thick greenery growing around the area, Uncle Ned had discovered old blackened pieces of logs lying there.

"How do you know it burned down, Uncle Ned?" Mandie asked. "Maybe this wood just rotted."

Uncle Ned reached down and crumbled the end of a log in his fingers. "Fire make ashes," he explained. "Like powder. Rot not make ashes."

The two young people bent to closely inspect the substance in Uncle Ned's hand.

"Yes, I can see it looks like powder," Mandie agreed.

"Besides, you can still smell the burn on the wood," Joe said. He picked up a small piece of wood to sniff it.

Mandie scanned the area. "I wonder what the cabin really looked like," she said. "I imagine it was romantic looking, surrounded by blooming flowers and trailing green vines, with the stream floating by, and fish swimming in the water."

Joe and Uncle Ned started examining the ground.

The old Indian scratched in the wet dirt and uncovered a corner of the stone hearth beneath the huge chimney. "Hearth here," Uncle Ned told them, pointing. Standing the axe by the chimney, he straightened up.

"And here are the pillars," Joe said, pulling the weeds away with the hoe. "You can tell how big the house was by these. See how far apart they are spaced? It was a good-sized house," he reasoned, pulling away weeds with the hoe to expose the stone pillars.

Mandie stroked Snowball as she explored the cabin ruins. "Here is where the front door was," Mandie called to them. "See, part of the steps is still here. Let me use the hoe, Joe."

The boy handed her the hoe and she beat down the weeds.

"Here spring house," Uncle Ned said, pointing to a clump of weeds. "Now that we find cabin, what Papoose do?"

"Nothing really, Uncle Ned," Mandie told him. "You see, this cabin was just one of the clues in the letters. Now that we know where it is, I would imagine the girl lived in the house where the school is now."

"But, Mandie, we aren't positive this is the cabin the man talked about in the letters," Joe reminded her. "All we've really found is what's left of some old house."

Mandie tossed her head. "I have a feeling, Joe, that this is the one," she replied. "Anyway, we'll say it is and work on the other clues from there."

The old Indian looked up at the sun through the thick trees. "Papoose go back now or be late," he said.

64

"I suppose it is about time to get back for supper," Mandie conceded. "Uncle Ned, we appreciate your finding the cabin for us. Thank you so much."

"Yes, thank you," Joe echoed.

"Papoose not do bad things, make trouble," he warned her. "Use head to think before body acts."

Mandie threw down the hoe and took her old friend's hand in her own. "I promise I won't get into any trouble, Uncle Ned," she said. "All we're going to do is ask some questions and try to find out who the girl was who received the letters."

"Uncle Ned is right, Mandie," Joe agreed. "I'm as curious about this as you are, but you've just got to stay out of trouble."

"All right, all right. Let's go," she said, picking up Snowball again. Turning quickly, they followed Uncle Ned as he led the way out of the woods back toward school.

At the bottom of the hill below the schoolhouse, Uncle Ned bid the two good-bye with a promise to return on the next change of the moon.

Mrs. Taft's buggy was waiting for Joe at the front steps.

Mandie gasped. "I hope I'm not late," she said. "Here, Joe, don't forget to take Snowball. See you tomorrow."

Handing him the kitten, she raced up the front steps as Joe got into the buggy to return to Mandie's grandmother's house.

Inside the hallway Mandie didn't see anyone about. Glancing at the big grandfather clock standing at the bottom of the stairs, she saw that she had plenty of time to get ready for supper.

She started up the steps and then stopped. It suddenly dawned on her that they had left the tools at the remains of the cabin. What if someone missed them?

They had already had them out since yesterday. She didn't want to get into trouble. *Maybe I should run back real fast and bring them back to the shed,* she thought, convinced she could find the way. Now that she knew where it was, it wouldn't take so long. *Yes, that's what I'd better do,* she decided.

Turning quickly, she ran back out the front door. Joe was already gone. With her heart pounding Mandie raced toward the woods. If she hurried she would be back in time to stay out of trouble.

Chapter 7 / What Happened to the Tools?

Mandie ran and ran until she was panting for breath. She brushed tree limbs and bushes out of her way and stumbled over the rough ground. Then a pain in her side slowed her down. Stopping by a huge chestnut tree to catch her breath for a moment, she suddenly thought she heard something in the thick woods. She could hardly hear anything except her own hard breathing, but somehow another sound caught her ear.

Her heart pounded. She stood perfectly still, trying to hold her breath as she listened. There it was again! Someone was tromping through the bushes. The noise grew fainter and then went off into the distance.

Mandie immediately hurried to her left in the direction of the old tumbled-down cabin. If she could only reach the clearing and grab the tools, she would have something to protect herself with, coming back.

She should be getting close. There was the faint sound of the creek. As she came into the clearing, she breathed a sigh of relief and ran to the place where she remembered dropping the hoe.

"Oh, where is it?" she cried to herself, looking all

around. "It's got to be here somewhere. Let's see, I was right here by the old steps, and Uncle Ned stood the axe by the chimney. Where is that hoe?"

Although she searched thoroughly for the hoe, it was not to be found. She circled the chimney. The axe had also disappeared. Someone had been there, evidently as soon as they left.

Mandie was really afraid now. Someone had those dangerous tools, and she was alone. The afternoon sunlight was growing dimmer inside the thick forest.

Clasping her hands in front of her, she looked through the treetops toward the barely visible sky.

"Dear Lord, what time I am afraid I will put my trust in Thee," she whispered aloud.

There, she thought, *God will see me safely back to the school. I don't have to worry anymore.* Taking a deep breath, she ran back into the trees and headed for the schoolhouse.

Without looking back or slowing down to listen for noises, she ran and ran until she came to the edge of the forest. Stumbling up the hill, she collapsed halfway to the top, out of breath.

She was safe now. The sun was still shining. The schoolhouse was in sight. Staring back at the forest while she regained her breath, she relaxed a little and didn't hear anyone approaching behind her. Suddenly there was a loud yell, and Mandie almost jumped out of her skin. Quickly turning around, she scrambled to her feet. When she saw it was only Celia running down the hill, she fell to the ground in relief.

Celia, a little short of breath from running, just stood there looking at Mandie.

"Oh, thank goodness it's you!" Mandie cried.

"If you don't hurry, you're going to be late for supper," Celia warned. "Come on, let's go!" Pulling Mandie up, she turned to go back up the hill with Mandie following.

At the top, arriving on level ground, Mandie questioned her friend. "Celia, when did you, and Miss Hope, and April get back?"

"A long time ago," Celia replied. "Miss Hope came back early. I looked everywhere around the school, but I couldn't find you, so I decided to walk down the hill, and there you were," she explained. "What happened?"

"I'm pretty sure we've found the cabin, Celia. But after Uncle Ned left and Joe went back to Grandmother's, I suddenly remembered we forgot to bring the tools back," Mandie explained, relating her adventures back through the woods alone.

Celia's eyes grew big as her friend told her about her journey into the woods, the noise she heard, and the disappearance of the tools.

"Mandie, please don't ever go back there again *alone*. Something might happen to you."

"Don't worry, I won't," Mandie promised.

Celia hugged her friend, and the girls hurried back to the house. "I suppose I must look a sight after going through all those bushes," Mandie said, reaching up to smooth her long blonde hair.

Celia stood back and looked at her. "Not really," she said. "You don't look as though you've been roaming through that forest. Just straighten your sleeves a little bit and tie your sash."

Mandie did as her friend suggested. Together they hurried down the hallway and joined the line of students as they were entering the dining room.

Almost bursting to swap details of their afternoon adventures, the girls quickly cleaned their plates and impatiently waited for everyone else to finish. When Miss Prudence stood and tinkled her little silver bell to dismiss the students, Celia and Mandie were the first ones through the door.

Rushing up the stairs, they collapsed across their bed.

"You first, Celia," Mandie said. "Tell me about the farm."

"It's enormous. Miss Hope said it has several thousand acres," Celia reported. "And most of it is used, for either cattle or crops. But there are a few acres of woods. And guess what?" she paused. "Uncle Cal's mother and his brother run the farm."

"They do?" Mandie looked confused. "Uncle Cal's mother must be awfully old."

"She's *real* old." Celia nodded. "They say she's still the boss out there, but her son really runs things. He's not as old as Uncle Cal."

"Did April behave?" Mandie asked.

"I suppose so," Celia replied. "She went off by herself as soon as we got there. Then on the way home she asked Miss Hope if it would be possible to bring some of the horses up to the school so the girls could take riding lessons," she said.

"April doesn't know how to ride? I'd imagined everyone knew how to ride a horse," Mandie mused.

Celia laughed. "I sure do. Horses are our family's business in Richmond, you know."

"Well, I guess some of these city slickers never learned," Mandie said.

Celia sat up on the bed. "Tell me what you and Joe and Uncle Ned did," she begged.

Mandie related all the details of the afternoon to her

friend, including the fact that Uncle Ned thought the cabin had burned down.

"So you think that's the cabin in the woods where the sweethearts used to meet?" Celia asked.

"Well, there's not much left of it, so I'm not positive. But I'm pretty sure." Mandie thought for a minute. "I just can't imagine who took the tools or why," she said, sitting up. "Why don't we try to talk to Miss Hope tonight? Her group must be finished with supper by now. Maybe we could ask her some questions."

Celia stood up. "I'm ready if you are," she replied.

The girls found Miss Hope in her office alone.

"May we come in, Miss Hope?" Mandie asked from the open doorway.

"Why, of course, girls. Come on in. Sit down," she invited.

"We just wanted to ask you about something that we're curious about," Mandie began.

"Yes, Amanda, what is it?" Miss Hope asked.

"You told us that you and Miss Prudence bought this house from a widow lady. Do you remember her name?" Mandie asked.

"Why, yes. She was Mrs. Scott," the schoolmistress answered, "I believe her whole name was Mrs. Hortense Howard Scott."

"Is she still living?" Celia asked.

Miss Hope thought for a moment. "I don't remember hearing of her death. In fact, we never saw her again after she left here," she said. "But she must be dead by now. That was forty-five years ago, and she was rather old *then*."

"Do you know if her daughter is still living? You told

us she had a daughter who married and left her alone," Mandie said.

"No, I'm sorry. I never met the daughter. In fact, I don't believe we even knew who she married, or where she lived. Mrs. Scott didn't go to live with her. She went to her sister's in Charlotte," the schoolmistress answered. "May I ask what brought on this sudden interest?"

"We were sorting all those things in the attic and we figured most of it must have been Mrs. Scott's. You said she left things here when she moved out," Mandie said.

"Yes, most of it did belong to Mrs. Scott. She told us they were things for which she no longer had any use, and she asked that we dispose of them. But we got busy and never really cleaned out the attic," Miss Hope explained.

"Are you and Miss Prudence the only ones who have actually lived here since you bought the house?" Mandie asked.

"Why, yes, except for the students," she replied.

Mandie cleared her throat nervously. "Miss Hope," she said in a rather shaky voice, "were you adopted?"

Miss Hope gasped in shock. "Adopted?"

"Yes, Ma'am," Celia answered.

"Why on earth would you ask me such a thing?" the schoolmistress asked.

"You and Miss Prudence don't look at all alike," Mandie told her. "We thought you might be adopted, or you and Miss Prudence might have different fathers, or something."

"Amanda, what are you saying?" the lady asked. "Different fathers?"

"I'm sorry, Miss Hope. I didn't mean anything bad." Mandie fumbled for words. "I meant that maybe your mother's husband died, and then she remarried, and you belonged to one husband and Miss Prudence to the other," she said, her face turning red.

"No, no!" Miss Hope replied. Rising quickly, she began tidying her desk. "Now if that's all you girls wanted to talk about, I'm sorry, but I have work to finish here."

The girls stood up.

"I'm sorry, Miss Hope. I know you're always busy," Mandie said.

Miss Hope smiled and said, "Never too busy to talk to you girls, Amanda."

"Thank you, Miss Hope," Mandie replied.

"We appreciate your time, Miss Hope. Good night," Celia added.

The girls returned to their room to rehash the conversation.

Mandie sat on the window seat in their room. "We didn't get much information, did we?" she said.

Celia plopped down beside her. "No, I guess not," she agreed. "Miss Hope did seem flustered when you asked her if she was adopted. What do you think?"

"I'd say she might have been adopted and didn't want us to know it for some reason. She did act a little nervous, and then right away she said she had work to do," Mandie said.

"I suppose if a person is adopted, they don't want to go around talking about it. I know I wouldn't," Celia confessed.

"I suppose," Mandie agreed. "Joe is coming back tomorrow at three-thirty. We'll see what he's got to say about solving this mystery in the letters."

"Where are the letters?" Celia asked suddenly.

"In the second bureau drawer where I put them last

night, remember?" Mandie said, going over to pull out the drawer.

"Celia, someone has been in here!" lamented Mandie. "Look at all the mess."

The letters *were* still there, but it was easy to see that someone had been rummaging through them.

Celia came up behind her and bent to get a closer look.

"It looks like someone took them all out of their envelopes," Celia said, picking up a handful of the papers. "See?"

"You're right," Mandie agreed. "Let's put them all back inside."

As the girls began carefully returning the fragile letters to their envelopes, Mandie spoke her thoughts aloud.

"I wonder who did this," she said. "Whoever has been snooping must have gotten into these letters after three-thirty. I opened the drawer to check on them just before I went downstairs to meet Joe this afternoon. They were all right then."

"We may never know who it was," Celia said.

"Well, I know one thing," Mandie said. "We're going to hide them this time."

"But where?" Celia asked.

Mandie thought for a moment. "Let me see," she said. "Hey, I know. We can put them all in an extra pillowcase and attach it to the back of the bureau where no one can see it."

"The back of the bureau? How are we going to do that?" Celia asked.

"I remember seeing some nails in the attic. I think the hammer is still up there, too. Let's go get them," Mandie said. "But first let's put these letters under our mattress till we get back."

The girls carefully hid the letters. Then carrying their oil lamp for light, they hurried upstairs to the attic to get the nails and hammer.

"Here they are," Mandie said, finding a paper bag of nails.

"And here's the hammer," Celia replied, picking it up.

"We only need two or three nails, so that's all I'll take," said Mandie. "We can bring the hammer back later."

Back in their room they retrieved the letters from under the mattress. Finding an extra pillowcase in a drawer, they stuffed the letters inside.

The big oak bureau was heavy, but with quite an effort, they were able to move it far enough away from the wall to tack a nail in the back side. Celia tied a knot in the top of the pillowcase, and they hung it on the nail.

"Whew!" Mandie said as they pushed the heavy bureau back into place. "This day has been full of hard work."

"You are right!" Celia agreed.

"I don't think anyone will find them now," Mandie said, satisfied with their work.

But no one else had to. Someone had already read them.

Chapter 8 / The Storm in the Graveyard

"Hello, Mandie. You and Celia are to come back with me to your grandmother's for supper tonight," Joe told the girls as he alighted from Mrs. Taft's buggy the next day. He handed Snowball to Mandie. "She sent a note to Miss Hope, and I have to give it to her. I'll be right back," he said, running inside.

Mandie rubbed Snowball's fur. "You have to behave this afternoon, Snowball. No running off. Do you hear?"

Celia stood next to Mandie and petted the little white kitten. "Mandie, I appreciate your grandmother always including me in her invitations," she said. "But maybe sometimes you might want to go to her house alone so you could talk together without me around."

"Oh, hush, Celia. Grandmother and I both want you to visit whenever I do," Mandie assured her. "After all, our mothers were friends here in this school together. Besides, you don't have any relatives near enough to visit."

Celia looked down to hide the tears of gratitude welling up in her pretty green eyes. "Thanks, Mandie," she said.

Mandie knew that Celia's mother hardly ever wrote to

her. She was still deeply grieving over her husband's sudden death. And Celia had no brothers or sisters.

Just then, Joe joined them on the porch. "Miss Hope said Uncle Cal will be waiting with the rig to take us to your grandmother's for supper at five o'clock," he informed the girls. "Now what are we doing this afternoon?"

"First we have to tell you what happened yesterday after you left," Mandie answered. "Come on. Let's walk down the hill so no one will hear us."

Laughing, the three raced to the edge of the woods and sat down on the grass. Mandie brought Joe up-to-date on the events of the day before.

"Somebody must have been watching us while we were there at the ruins of that old cabin," Joe said. "Then they took the tools as soon as we left, I suppose."

"That's what we thought, too," Mandie replied. "But I can't imagine who it was or how we could ever find out."

"Someone also opened all the letters while they were in the bureau drawer in our room," Celia added.

"Oh, no!" Joe moaned. "You mean someone read them?"

"Evidently," Mandie said. "They were all out of their envelopes and unfolded when we looked in the drawer after supper last night."

"I'd say someone is definitely trying to find out what we're so interested in," Joe remarked, breaking off blades of grass as he sat there.

"Well, are we going to the cabin?" Celia asked. "Remember, I haven't even seen it yet."

Mandie jumped up and dusted herself off. "Of course, Celia. Let's go," she said.

Agreeing to listen for anyone else who might be in

the woods, the three tramped silently through the underbrush straight to the site of the tumbled-down cabin.

As they came out into the clearing, Celia excitedly ran over to the remains of the old cabin.

"Is this it?" she asked, looking around at the fallen timbers and the tall chimney.

"We *think* this is the cabin they talked about in the letters," Mandie said. "Or what is left of it."

"Oh, isn't it sad? This is all that's left of that beautiful love story," Celia said, picking her way though the weeds as she looked about.

Joe laughed. "Don't get so sentimental over it. This might not even be the place in the letters," he reminded her.

"But if we can put other pieces of the puzzle together, I think we can find out for sure," Mandie said.

"Why don't we see what else is around here in these woods?" Joe suggested.

"Let's do!" exclaimed Mandie.

"Yes," Celia agreed.

Joe started walking over to the creek bank. "Let's follow the creek and see where it goes," he said.

The three young people pushed their way through the heavy underbrush, wandering still farther from the schoolhouse. Here and there birds flitted excitedly from branch to branch. Squirrels ran up tree trunks and sat there, peeping from behind limbs to watch the intruders.

Although unnoticed by the three young people, it began to grow darker. The sun disappeared behind the trees. The forest seemed to go on forever. Then way in the distance they spotted a high rock wall.

"Look!" cried Mandie, pointing ahead.

The three stopped and stared at each other. Breaking

into a run, they rushed to investigate.

As they got close to the wall, they could see a big iron gate in the center. "It's a cemetery," Mandie whispered, stroking Snowball.

Joe walked toward the gate and pushed it open. "Let's go inside," he said.

The girls followed. Inside, weeds grew thick and wild around tumbled-down tombstones. Huge trees stood like guards watching over the dead, and an old stone building cowered in the corner.

Celia hesitated at the gateway. "We can't walk in there," she protested. "It's too grown up with weeds and things."

"Oh, come on, Celia," Mandie urged. "It's no worse than what we've been through in the woods." She walked on ahead and Celia timidly followed. Joe hurried from one grave to another, trying to read the faded inscriptions on some of the weather-worn stones.

Mandie tried to keep up with him but paused to pull weeds away from some of the stones along the way. "If we got some water and scrubbed these stones, I think we could read some of the names," she suggested.

Joe stopped. "Where would we get water?" he asked.

"The creek, of course. We've been walking by it all the way," Mandie reminded him.

"How are we going to carry it? In your apron?" Joe teased.

The two girls laughed.

"I don't suppose we could find a bucket, or something like that," Mandie said.

"I sure haven't seen one lying around anywhere," Joe replied. "Besides, that would take too long."

Suddenly a heavy wind swooped down through the graveyard, nearly blowing the three young people over.

Lightning flashed. Thunder cracked. They grabbed each other in fright. Snowball dug his claws into Mandie's shoulder.

"It's blowing up a storm!" Joe yelled above the roar. "We'd better head for the school!"

The girls nodded and held hands tightly as they turned to leave the cemetery. Just then the clouds opened up and unloaded torrents of rain.

Joe pulled at Mandie's hand. "Over here!" he cried, pulling them in the direction of the stone building in the corner.

Instantly drenched by the rain, the girls hurried behind him until they reached the building. They froze in their tracks. It was a tomb!

Joe tried to get the door open.

Mandie screamed. "N-not in th-there, Joe!" she cried.

"Oh, come on," he insisted, tugging at the door with one hand and pulling at Mandie with the other. The door jerked open, and he pushed the girls inside, out of the rain.

Snowball had been good all afternoon, but now he meowed loudly as he licked his fur, trying to dry himself.

Mandie held her kitten tightly and huddled together with Celia. It was dark inside. Both girls were shivering, and they refused to budge from the step inside the doorway.

Joe walked around inside and came back to report. "Nothing here," he said. "Just some old dead people. They can't hurt us."

"Joe, stop it!" Mandie cried, her voice quivering from fright and cold.

Celia was already shaking in real terror, then suddenly something touched her hair in the darkness. She screamed and ran outside into the rain.

Joe dashed after her. "Stop, Celia! It was just an old grasshopper that got in your hair," he told her, pulling at her hand. "Come back in out of the rain."

"A-a g-g-grass-h-hopper?" she cried, finally standing still while the rain beat down on both of them.

"Yes, you've seen hundreds of grasshoppers I'm sure. Come on. We're getting drenched," he told her.

Reluctantly, Celia let Joe guide her back inside the tomb to join Mandie right inside the doorway.

Mandie grasped Joe's other hand while he still held onto Celia's. "We need to ask for protection!" Mandie yelled above the roar. She turned her face upward.

Joe and Celia understood.

Holding hands together, they recited Mandie's favorite prayer. " 'What time I am afraid I will put my trust in Thee.' "

The three smiled at each other, unable to speak.

Outside, the storm raged on. They could hear lightning striking trees. The wind roared as though it were sweeping the whole cemetery away.

The three young people huddled together, their hearts beating wildly. Snowball clung to Mandie's shoulder, meowing in fright.

Then as suddenly as it had come, the storm moved on. The three young people rushed outside in relief. Sunshine filtered through the thick trees. Snowball still clung desperately as Mandie turned to close the door behind them. Only then did she notice the name inscribed on the door.

"Scott! These people were Scotts!" she cried excitedly.

"Let's get out of here!" yelled Celia, running through the wet grass and weeds toward the gate.

"We'd better hurry," Joe agreed.

All three of them were soaking wet. The girls' long, heavy skirts hindered them as they made their way back through the woods to the school. No one said anything. They were in too big of a hurry and too much out of breath for that. As they came to a clearing on the hillside below the school, they could see the rig tied to the hitching post at the front steps.

"We're late!" Mandie cried.

"And in trouble!" Celia added.

Joe tried to help the girls up the hillside, but he was wet, too, and progress was slow. As they reached the front porch, Miss Hope came outside.

"My goodness! You were caught in the storm!" she exclaimed. "Girls, run upstairs quickly and change into dry clothes. Joe, I'm afraid I don't have a thing for you to wear. I trust you won't catch a cold before you get back to Amanda's grandmother's house to change."

"We'll be right back," Mandie told Joe. She and Celia hurried through the doorway and up the stairs to their room.

Joe sat on the steps and talked to Miss Hope.

"Where were y'all? Couldn't you find shelter anywhere?" Miss Hope asked.

"No, ma'am," Joe said. "You see, we were in the cemetery in the woods, and by the time we managed to get inside the vault there, we were drenched to the skin."

"Cemetery?" Miss Hope asked. "Where is this cemetery? I don't remember ever seeing one around here."

"It's way on the other side of the creek beyond the woods down there," he explained.

"Oh, that's not our land," Miss Hope said. "We only bought the acreage up to the creek when we got the house. I don't really know who owns that land now. I don't think it has ever been used while we've been living here," she told him.

"The vault was the only shelter we could find from the rain," Joe said. Then smiling mischievously, he added, "Of course, the girls didn't want to go inside the vault. They were afraid."

"I don't blame them at all," Miss Hope said.

"It's my fault that we're late, Miss Hope. I suggested exploring the woods," he told her.

"We'll overlook it this time," the schoolmistress said. "The good Lord himself must have helped protect you."

Just then Mandie and Celia appeared on the porch in dry dresses, their damp hair combed back and tied with ribbons. Uncle Cal stood behind them.

"Miss Hope, I'm sorry we were late," Mandie apologized.

"Me, too, Miss Hope," Celia added.

"Don't worry about it this time. I just hope y'all don't get colds from this. Now hurry on. Your grandmother will be worried, Amanda, if you are too late," the schoolmistress said. "Uncle Cal, hurry back."

As soon as they arrived at Mrs. Taft's, Joe quickly changed into dry clothes. Then they all went in to enjoy the supper waiting on the dining table.

During the meal, the young people related their adventures to Mrs. Taft and Dr. Woodard but did not mention the letters they had found in the trunk.

"So you got caught in the rain," Mrs. Taft said. "And then had to stand in a vault to wait it out? My, my! That must have been eerie!"

"It sure wasn't fun!" Mandie declared, helping herself to more roast beef. "Grandmother, did you ever know the

Mrs. Scott who owned the big house that is our school now?" she asked.

"That was a long time ago, Amanda," her grandmother reminded her. "We weren't living here then. In fact, we were still in Franklin when your mother went to school there. We didn't move to Asheville until about twelve years ago."

"Did you know them, Dr. Woodard?" Mandie asked.

"Well, no. I can't say I did," the doctor replied. "I do remember hearing the name years ago. It seems like Mr. Scott was a right well-to-do man. He owned a lot of land and mica mines, I believe."

"Mica mines?" questioned Celia.

"You know," Mandie said, "that shiny stuff they dig out of the ground. You can see yourself in it, like a mirror," she explained.

"And it's in layers?" Celia asked.

"That's it," Mandie told her. "Dr. Woodard, you didn't personally know them?" she asked.

"No, but I remember my father mentioning Mr. Scott. You see, my father was a doctor here in Asheville," Dr. Woodard replied. "That was ages ago."

"I didn't know your father was a doctor," Mandie said.

"And the older Dr. Woodard was a friend of your grandfather's, Amanda," Mrs. Taft added.

"I suppose everybody knew everybody back then," Mandie said.

Dr. Woodard eyed her curiously. "Why were you interested in the Scotts?" he asked.

"Miss Hope said they bought the house from a Mrs. Scott, and then the vault we hid in this afternoon had the name Scott on it. I just thought it might be the same family," Mandie explained.

"It probably is if the cemetery is not too far from the school," the doctor said.

As dessert was served, Dr. Woodard changed the subject. "Well, are you young folks coming with me to see Hilda Saturday, or did you have something else planned?"

"Oh, yes, Dr. Woodard, I'd love to go," Mandie replied.

"I would, too," Celia answered.

Mrs. Taft seemed pleased that Mandie and Celia were still interested in the young retarded girl. "I'll send the rig over for you girls Friday afternoon, then. You can spend the weekend here," she said with delight.

The three young people looked at each other silently. Mandie thought about how they wanted to explore other clues in the letters. They wouldn't have a chance to do that while staying at her grandmother's house. But what else could they do? They would have to come and visit as her grandmother asked.

Later, in the sitting room, the three young people discussed the situation while the adults had coffee in the dining room.

"We'll just have to bring the letters with us," Mandie said. "Maybe if we read them all over again, we can find some more clues."

"I'd like to hunt for the diamonds the man mentions in the letters." Joe's eyes twinkled. "Now that we think we've found the cabin in the woods, maybe we could track down those diamonds."

"Good idea!" Celia agreed.

"We'll concentrate on that next," Mandie decided.

Someone else was also concentrating on that.

Chapter 9 / Treasures from Long Ago

Friday afternoon Mandie, Celia, and Joe set off for the tumbled-down cabin in the woods. They had all reread the letters and had decided the best thing to do next was to go over the area inch by inch. If the cabin had burned down, there was the possibility that the contents of the house had been scattered nearby.

"Let's split up," Joe said. "Mandie, you begin in that corner over there by the creek and, Celia, you start at that corner over there. I'll work back and forth between these other two corners."

"Don't forget to watch for any stakes, or unusual rocks," Mandie reminded her friends.

"Or there could be some old paths beneath all these weeds," Celia said.

"I can move the logs for you when you get to them," Joe told the girls.

They worked in silence for a long time without finding anything unusual.

Then suddenly, Celia squealed in excitement as she bent over, examining something at her feet. "Hey! Come here!" she cried. "I've found something!"

Mandie and Joe raced to her side. Celia was trying to open a wooden box that had the lid smashed shut.

"Let me find something to hit that with," Joe said. He looked around and picked up a heavy board. "Get back. Let me take a whack at it."

He beat and banged, turning the box at different angles. Finally the lid flew open, and the young people gathered closer to look inside.

"Looks like some old clothes," Joe said, pulling a long piece of black cloth from the box.

"A scarf," Celia corrected him.

"There's something else," Mandie said. She reached inside and pulled out a shiny object. "It's a picture!" she said, holding up a small oval frame, covered with grime.

Using the end of the black scarf, Mandie vigorously wiped the frame clean enough to reveal the picture of a beautiful girl with dark curls and laughing eyes.

"Look!" Mandie handed the picture to Celia.

Celia took it and sighed. "Oh, how sad!" she said. "This must be the girl who received the letters!"

"Probably, but we don't know for sure," Joe persisted.

Mandie kept rummaging in the box. "Here's a handkerchief," she said, holding up a small, dirty piece of white linen and lace. "I suppose these things were her sweetheart's keepsakes."

"That's all that's in there," Joe said. "I wonder why the box wasn't scorched."

"It might not have been inside the cabin," Mandie suggested. "Anyway, we'd better hurry and finish."

Although they inspected the entire open area around where the cabin once stood, they found nothing else.

"Looks like the only thing to do is dig," Joe commented. He sat down on a fallen log.

"Dig? You mean dig up this whole place? Why that would take forever," Mandie told him.

"That's the only way to find anything else. The cabin has been burned down so long the weeds have probably covered what was left," the boy replied.

"We don't have any tools any more, remember?" Celia reminded her friends. "Whoever took them never did bring them back."

"We can borrow Grandmother's," Mandie said. "And speaking of Grandmother, I imagine it's about time to get back to school. We have to go to her house tonight for the weekend, you know. Celia, will you bring that picture, and the handkerchief, and scarf with you?"

Celia picked up the objects and followed Mandie along the path. Joe brought up the rear.

Ben had Mrs. Taft's rig waiting when they arrived back at the school. Leaving Joe downstairs, the girls ran to their room and grabbed their already-packed bags.

"Let's get the letters," Mandie said. "We can put these things we've found into the pillowcase with the letters and take it all to Grandmother's house. That way we'll know where things are."

"Good idea," Celia said.

The girls pulled the bureau away from the wall enough to reach behind and get the pillowcase containing the letters. Celia dropped the picture, handkerchief, and scarf into the pillowcase with the letters. Then Mandie stuffed the whole thing under her books in the school bag she was taking to her grandmother's house.

"Now we know everything is safe," Mandie said. At the last moment she grabbed a red dress from the chifferobe and tossed the dress into her bag.

"For Hilda," she explained, as Celia looked at her questioningly.

Hurrying back downstairs with their bags, the girls found Miss Hope in her office and told her good-bye. Then they joined Joe in the rig for the ride to Mrs. Taft's house.

On Saturday, Dr. Woodard took the three young people to see the mentally retarded girl they had found hiding in the school's attic.

As they rode down the cobblestone streets on their way to the private sanitarium, Mandie questioned him. "You say Hilda has never said a word to anyone, Dr. Woodard?"

"Not one word," the doctor replied. "We still don't know whether she is even capable of speaking, but otherwise her health has improved considerably."

When they arrived at the sanitarium, Hilda was brought to the parlor to visit with her friends. Mandie and Celia hardly recognized her. She had gained weight and was neatly dressed. Her shiny, long brown hair was tied back with a ribbon.

Hilda stared at Mandie and the others. Then a faint smile brightened her face.

Mandie reached into her bag, pulled out the red dress that she had brought her, and cautiously approached the girl. Hilda stood still. When Mandie held out the dress to her, she smiled broadly and took it. Holding it up against herself, she turned this way and that, admiring the dress.

"Remember us?" Mandie asked her. "I'm Mandie, this is Celia, and that's Joe. And you know Dr. Woodard, I'm sure."

Hilda looked at the dress and then at Mandie. With a sudden rush, she put her arms around Mandie and hugged her tightly.

"Thank you!" Hilda whispered, barely audibly.

Mandie whirled to look at the others.

She spoke! "Thank the Lord! She spoke! She said 'thank you.' She can talk!" Mandie cried excitedly. She turned back to embrace the girl. "Oh, Hilda, you can talk! Praise the Lord!"

Hilda nodded her head as tears ran down her cheeks.

Dr. Woodard walked over to Hilda, took her arm, and guided her to the chair nearby.

"Here, sit down, Hilda," he said gently. "You don't have to cry about it. We're all happy. And when you're happy, you should smile and laugh, not cry."

Hilda wiped her eyes with the back of her hand and smiled.

Mandie leaned down in front of the girl and held her hands. "Hilda, what else can we bring you?" she asked.

Celia and Joe stood beside Mandie.

"Hilda, we'll bring you anything else you'd like," Celia offered.

"Would you like another ribbon for your hair?" Joe asked.

The young people continued to talk to Hilda, but she would not say another word. She just sat there smiling at them and hugging the dress Mandie had given her.

"We don't want to tire her out," Dr. Woodard said. "I think we'd better go now. I'll bring you back next time I come to Asheville."

The young people said good-bye to Hilda but she just sat there smiling. As they drove off in the rig Mandie smiled and looked up into the blue cloudless sky. "Thank you, dear God, thank you. Hilda can speak," she said quietly.

"That is indeed something to thank God for," Dr. Woodard said. "Now that we know she's capable of speaking, we'll try to help her start talking."

Mandie looked up into the doctor's kind face. "I don't know if it was a miracle that she spoke those two words or if she really knows how to talk, but I've been praying for her, Dr. Woodard. I think more prayers can still accomplish a lot more," she said.

"Prayers can work wonders," the doctor replied.

At the supper table that night, Mandie asked her grandmother about borrowing some tools.

"A hoe? A rake and a shovel? What on earth do you and Celia want with such things?" her grandmother asked.

"We'd like to do a little digging," Mandie said with a secretive smile.

"Digging? Well, I suppose you will need tools to do any digging," Mrs. Taft answered. "But, mind you, don't do anything that will cause trouble at school and bring your mother down on our heads. I can handle Miss Prudence, but your mother is a different story."

Mandie laughed. "We won't, Grandmother. We promise."

"When we get finished here, Amanda, go find Ben and tell him I said to put a hoe, a rake and a shovel in the rig when he takes y'all back to school tomorrow," Mrs. Taft told the girl.

"Thank you, Grandmother," Mandie said.

Joe and Celia smiled as they caught Mandie's glance. When they returned to school, they would have the necessary tools to continue their search in the woods for the diamonds.

As they drove up in the rig the next night, Uncle Cal was just coming down the front steps of the schoolhouse.

Mandie jumped down and called to him. "Uncle Cal!

Would you please do something for us?"

The old man came over to the rig.

"Why, yes, Missy," he said.

Mandie pointed to the tools on the floorboard of the rig.

"Would you please take these tools over to your house before anyone sees them? We borrowed them from my Grandmother, and we'll be over tomorrow afternoon to get them," Mandie explained.

"Lawsy mercy, Missy. Why y'all bring dese when we got sech things right heah?" he asked, picking up the tools.

"But, Uncle Cal, the school's tools disappeared after we used them," Mandie told him.

"Didn't y'all know dey back in de shed? 'Cause dat where dey be," he said, looking from one to another of the young people.

"No," the three said in unison.

"When did you see them there, Uncle Cal?" Joe asked.

"Why I notices 'em yistiddy, I reckons," the old man said. "After I sees Missy April leave de shed, I goes inside and sees de tools be back." He looked around to see if anyone was watching. "Now lemme go fo' somebody done sees us. I leaves dese unduh de front porch fo' you." He walked away quickly, carrying the tools.

"Well, at least we'll have plenty to dig with." Joe squeezed Mandie's hand. "See you tomorrow afternoon," he said. "Good night." Jumping back into the rig, he rode off with Ben.

Mandie and Celia hurried into the schoolhouse.

"So someone brought the tools back, and April Snow was down at the shed. That really puzzles me," Mandie said as the two girls entered their room.

Celia began unpacking her school bag. "At least we won't get in trouble for losing the school's tools," she said, not realizing how much trouble still lay ahead.

Chapter 10 / Hidden Diamonds

"We'll only need the tools we brought from Grandmother's house," Mandie told Joe and Celia the next afternoon. "There are only three of us, so we can use only three tools at a time."

"You're right," Joe agreed. Stooping to locate the tools under Uncle Cal's front porch, he reached under and pulled them out.

Celia picked up the rake. "May I use this?" she asked. "I rake better than I hoe."

"Sure," Mandie replied. "I'll take the hoe and leave you the shovel, Joe."

"Let's get out of sight with these tools before someone stops us," Joe urged, leading the way down the hillside toward the woods.

Arriving at the clearing where the cabin had stood, the three young people began their search. With great enthusiasm, they hoed, raked and shoveled, but they found nothing more than some old rusty nails.

Disgusted, Joe sat down on the cracked hearth to rest. "That was a lot of work for nothing," Joe said, glancing over the clean ground. Taking off his shoes, he shook out the dirt that had filtered inside.

Celia began swinging her bonnet for a fan. "I don't know when I've worked so hard," she admitted. "I guess I'm not very good with a rake either." She laughed.

Mandie wiped the perspiration from her brow and took off her bonnet. "I can't believe we haven't found anything," she said. "This has to be the place." With a sigh, she plopped herself down next to Joe on the cracked hearth.

Celia joined her. "Where would you hide diamonds if you had some?" she asked her two friends.

Joe thought for a moment. "I'd probably pull up a floor board and put them under there," he answered. "But you see, we've dug all around where the floor of the cabin must have been."

"I'd probably stick them up the chimney," Mandie said.

"The chimney? Wouldn't they ruin from the heat?" Celia asked.

"I don't think so, but I don't really know," Joe replied.

"Then what about the hearth? Under the hearth?" Mandie asked. Suddenly she stood up. "The hearth! We haven't looked under the hearth!" she exclaimed.

Joe frowned at her. "How would you hide something under a hearth?" he asked.

He and Celia stood up to examine what they had been sitting on.

"It *is* cracked," Celia observed.

"Maybe it was cracked on purpose so part of it could be pulled up," Mandie cried. "Let's dig it up."

Picking up her hoe, Mandie started banging at the hearth.

Joe took the hoe from her. "Here. I can do that faster than you can," he said.

Joe dug away at the crack until gradually the stone hearth fell apart. There seemed to be nothing but dirt under it. Then the hoe hit something that made a clinking sound.

"There's something there!" Mandie cried.

"Don't get too close. I might accidentally hit you while I'm swinging this thing," Joe warned the girls.

He quickly dug the dirt out of the spot until something metal showed through. As he pushed the dirt aside, the girls squealed with joy at the sight of a small metal box.

"At last!" Joe exclaimed.

Mandie jumped up and down. "This has got to be the diamonds!" she said excitedly.

"It's got to be!" Celia echoed.

Joe pulled the box out of the dirt and set it on the remaining piece of hearth. He tried to open it, but the lid was wedged tightly shut.

"Get back," he cautioned. "I'm going to beat it open with the hoe."

After a few blows the lid flew open, revealing a candy box similar to the one in which they had found the letters. The girls crowded around as Joe opened the candy box. Inside, on a bed of black velvet, lay a set of wedding rings. sparkling with diamonds in the sunlight.

Joe gasped. "Wedding rings!"

The three plopped down on the ground and laughed till their sides hurt.

"Why, of course!" Mandie said when she could catch her breath. "Why didn't we figure that out? They hid the wedding rings here."

"Wedding rings," Joe murmured. "And here I thought

I was hunting for diamonds."

"But these are diamonds," Celia told him, pointing to one of the rings. "Look. There must be a dozen diamonds in that one ring alone."

"Now that we've found them, we know this is the cabin in the woods that the man wrote about in the letters," Mandie said.

"Yes, and now that we've found them, would you please tell me what you're going to do with them?" Joe asked.

"We'll take them back to our room until we can decide what to do next," Mandie replied.

Celia kept staring at the beautiful rings. "We still need to figure out who they belong to," she said.

"I have an idea those rings have been here for many, many years. Those letters must be old as the hills," Joe said.

"How are we going to get them to our room without anyone seeing us?" Celia asked.

Mandie thought for a moment. "When we get to the edge of the woods I'll take my bonnet off and cover the box with it," she suggested.

"You'd better be careful," Joe warned her. "That will look suspicious, carrying your bonnet to hide something."

He started pushing the pieces of the hearth back into place as much as he could and the girls helped.

Then Mandie suggested a plan. "Uncle Cal is going to take you back to Grandmother's, Joe," she said. "So if you and Celia can get the tools back under his house, I'll rush up to our room with the rings," Mandie planned. "Will you tell Uncle Cal to take the tools back to Grandmother's when he takes you?"

"Sure," Joe agreed.

Everything worked out according to plan, and Mandie took the box of rings up to their room. When Celia came upstairs the two girls pulled the bureau out and added the box to the contents of the pillowcase on the back.

Mandie started out the door. "I guess we'd better both run for the bathroom to get cleaned up," she said.

"I know the bell's going to ring any minute for supper," Celia agreed, following her friend down the hallway to the bathroom.

Mandie hastily washed up. "I sure hope we can find out who wrote those letters," she said.

"Me, too," Celia replied, washing her face and hands. "I'd like to know who those diamonds belonged to. It's really sad when you think about finding those old letters and then finding the diamond rings and the handkerchief with the picture. They must have really been in love, and for some reason they never got married."

Mandie dusted off her shoes. "I'm going to have to change if we have time," she said. "My dress is dirty around the hem from digging in the dirt all afternoon."

Celia inspected her own dress. "Maybe we should," she advised. Hurriedly opening the door of the bathroom, they came face to face with April Snow who was sitting on the window seat across the hallway from the door.

Mandie paused a second in surprise and then rushed down the hallway to their room. Celia quickly followed.

"Why was she sitting there of all places," Mandie wondered aloud. Grabbing a clean dress from the chifferobe, she moved out of the way for Celia to get one. They quickly unbuttoned the backs of their dirty dresses and took them off, slipping the clean dresses over their heads.

"I don't know why she was there," Celia answered,

fastening her dress, "but I hope she didn't hear what we were saying in the bathroom."

"I'll just bet she was listening at the door, and when she heard us start to leave, she probably rushed over to the window seat," Mandie looked at Celia with concern.

"Well, let her listen. She can't figure out what we were talking about because everything is well hidden now," Celia said.

The bell rang for supper, and the girls looked in the tall floor-length mirror in the corner. They rushed out into the hallway, unaware of the pair of eyes that watched them from behind the window draperies in the hall.

Later, as the girls left the dining room, Uncle Cal met them in the hallway. The girls stopped to talk.

"Hello, Uncle Cal," Mandie said.

Celia smiled broadly. "I keep forgetting to tell you that I met your mother and your brother the other day when I went out to the school's farm," she said.

"You did?" The old Negro laughed. "Phoebe, she got to go out theah tomorrow," he said.

"Your mother seemed awfully old to be working so hard," Celia said.

"Yessum, Missy. She be ol'. She done be workin' fo' Miz Prudence and Miz Hope for nigh onto forty-six years now," he said.

"Forty-six years!" exclaimed Mandie as something nudged her memory. "Uncle Cal, did she work here at the school?"

"Yessum, Missy. She wuz workin' heah befo' Miz Prudence and Miz Hope gets dis house. She work heah till me and Phoebe come. Den she go to de farm," the old man explained.

"She did!" Mandie's eyes grew wide. "And Aunt Phoebe

is going to see her tomorrow. May we go, too, Uncle Cal?" Mandie asked excitedly.

Celia, realizing the impact of all this information, joined in. "We sure would like to go," she said.

"Y'all hafta aks Miz Prudence or Miz Hope," Uncle Cal said. "Phoebe, she ain't got to go till late tomorrow. Maybe suppuhtime."

"Please tell Aunt Phoebe that we'll ask for permission to go with her," Mandie instructed.

"I'll sho' do dat, Missy," Uncle Cal said, continuing his way down the hallway.

"What a break!" Mandie whispered to her friend.

"Yes, if we're allowed to go," Celia replied. "Joe is coming back tomorrow afternoon, remember?"

"We'll send him back to Grandmother's if he comes before Aunt Phoebe leaves," Mandie suggested. "Otherwise we'll send word for him not to come. He'll understand."

Mandie and Celia waited until they were sure those at the second sitting were finished with supper, then they went downstairs to look for Miss Hope in her office.

As they came to her opened door, they froze in shock. Miss Hope was sitting at her desk, opening the candy box with the rings in it!

They remained motionless in the dim hallway.

"Celia!" Mandie gasped.

"Miss Hope has the rings!" Celia whispered, huddling close to her friend to avoid being seen.

Miss Hope took the rings out of the box and sat there staring at them. "What in the world?" she said to herself, turning the rings over and over in her hand. She carefully examined the candy box, then looked up and saw Mandie and Celia standing in the hallway. Quickly dropping the rings back into the box, she closed it as she rose.

"Did you girls want something?" she asked.

Mandie and Celia slowly approached her, trying to pretend they hadn't seen anything.

"Miss Hope, may we have permission to go to the farm with Aunt Phoebe tomorrow?" Mandie asked.

"To the farm? With Aunt Phoebe?" Miss Hope questioned. "Aunt Phoebe isn't leaving until late in the afternoon, and it will probably be dark by the time she gets back. I'm sure she will be gone during suppertime."

"That's all right, Miss Hope," Mandie replied. "We'd just like to go with her. I haven't seen the farm yet, you know."

"I suppose you two could eat supper at the farm with Aunt Phoebe. Neither one of you has classes at that time of day. But what about your friend, Joe? Isn't he coming here tomorrow for your afternoon free period?" Miss Hope asked.

"Oh, that's all right. We'll just tell Joe we're going away for the afternoon and won't be here," Mandie said. "He won't mind."

"You may go if you girls promise to be on your best behavior," Miss Hope instructed. "I know Aunt Phoebe is awfully lenient with you two."

"Thank you, Miss Hope. You can trust us to behave like young ladies should in every way," Mandie promised.

"Yes, Miss Hope, we will," Celia added.

Miss Hope looked at them a little skeptically. "I'll let her know y'all are going with her," she said.

The girls excused themselves and practically ran to their room to check on the letters and other articles in the pillowcase. Everything was as they had left it except for the missing rings.

"We might as well take all this and put it somewhere else. Obviously, someone has found it and taken the rings," Mandie said.

The girls laid everything on their bed and slid the bureau back in place.

"I'm worried about those rings," Mandie continued. "How in the world did Miss Hope get them?"

"I don't know, but I'd say there's no way for us to get them back," Celia said. "Why don't we put the letters and everything else in your trunk or mine and lock it up?"

"Good idea," Mandie agreed.

Each of the girls had a small trunk sitting in the corner of their room.

Mandie took the pillowcase full of clues over to her trunk and put everything inside. Locking it up she pinned the key inside her apron pocket. "That's got to be safe now," she said.

"But someone has probably read the letters already," Celia reminded her.

"And someone found our hiding place. I don't understand how Miss Hope could have the rings, but at least we know where they are. We'll just have to find out how they got there," Mandie concluded.

Chapter 11 / Aunt Pansy Tells It All

The next afternoon, Mandie and Celia were waiting for Joe on the veranda when he arrived in Mrs. Taft's buggy.

"Joe! Tell Ben to wait a minute," Mandie called as Joe alighted from the buggy.

Joe did as she said and then quickly ran up the steps. "What's the matter?" he asked.

"Wait till you hear our news!" Mandie began.

"Sit down a minute," Celia said, motioning toward the porch swing.

Mandie tried to choose her words carefully. "Joe, would you mind going back with Ben? We're going away this afternoon," Mandie said.

Joe looked puzzled. "Where?" he asked.

"We're going to the school farm with Aunt Phoebe in a little while," Mandie explained. "Let me tell you what's going on."

The three sat in the swing while Mandie related the events of the day before. She told him about the rings turning up on Miss Prudence's desk, and the fact that Uncle Cal's mother had worked for the Scotts.

Joe listened intently. "Couldn't I go to the farm with you?" he asked.

"No, I'm sure they wouldn't allow that," Mandie replied. "We told Miss Hope we didn't think you'd mind going back to Grandmother's. I wish you could go with us, but if you can come back tomorrow afternoon, we'll let you know everything we find out."

Joe pretended to be hurt. "This isn't fair!" he teased. "I'm working on this mystery, too." He laughed and flipped Mandie's long blonde hair.

"I know, Joe. But if we start asking for too many favors, Miss Hope might decide we can't go," Mandie explained.

Just then, Aunt Phoebe came out the door and put her hands on her hips. "Come on, Missies, we'se ready to go," she told the girls.

Mandie and Celia quickly rose and followed her into the house.

"We'll see you tomorrow afternoon, Joe," Mandie called back. "I'm sorry you can't go."

"So am I," Joe said, looking a little dejected as he walked down the steps to join Ben in the buggy again.

The girls followed Aunt Phoebe out the back door where the rig was waiting, and soon they were on their way to the farm.

Aunt Phoebe shook her head. "I don't know why y'all wants to miss dat suppuh at de school to go to de country and eat beans and cornbread," she said as she urged the horse down the country road.

"Beans and cornbread? That's the best food I know of," Mandie said excitedly. "I haven't had that kind of a supper since I lived with my father in Swain County."

Celia frowned. "Is that all we'll have, Aunt Phoebe?" she asked.

"Well, reckon we mought have buttermilk and some sweet cake," the old woman told her.

"That sounds better." Celia smiled.

Mandie's head was full of questions. "What's Uncle Cal's mother's name?" she asked.

"Huh name be Pansy—Aunt Pansy Jones," Phoebe replied.

"Pansy? That's a beautiful name. Is Jones your last name, too?" Mandie asked.

"It sho' be. It be Jones evuh since I got hitched up with Cal," the Negro woman said. "And dat be a long time ago."

They had come to a fence along the road, and the old woman stopped the rig. "Well, heah we be," she said, starting to get down to open the gate.

"Let me, Aunt Phoebe," Mandie cried.

Excitedly, she jumped down and swung the gate open. The rig went through and stopped to wait for her. Carefully closing the gate again, she ran to get back into the rig.

"You sho' know how to do dat, Missy," the old woman said.

"Of course, I do. Remember, I was raised on a farm," replied Mandie.

As Aunt Phoebe drove the rig up a winding dirt road, Mandie looked around at the rows and rows of crops growing in the fields and at the large outbuildings along the way. "This must be a huge farm," she said.

"Sho is," the old woman muttered. She pulled the rig up in front of a stable. "De house be up dat away." She pointed up the hill at a clump of trees.

Stepping down into the yard, Aunt Phoebe started to lead the girls up the hill.

"Is that where Aunt Pansy lives?" Mandie asked.

"Yes, Mandie." Celia answered. "I met her when I was here the other day."

"She lib up deah, an' so do Cal's brothuh, Rufus," Aunt Phoebe said.

A tall, young black boy came out of the stables and took the reins of the horse.

Aunt Phoebe turned around. "You git dem vittles loaded. We be leavin' right aftuh suppuh. You hears me, Jimson?"

"Yessum, Miz Phoebe," the boy said. He turned to stare curiously at the girls as they walked up the hill.

Mandie hurried ahead as she spied the house. "A log cabin!" she cried, running up the hill.

The big old log cabin seemed to sit in the middle of a colorful flower garden edged with green shrubbery and gigantic trees.

A huge old Negro woman stood on the porch watching the three approach.

When Mandie saw her, she ran up the steps. "Aunt Pansy, I'm Mandie—Amanda, they call me at school," she introduced herself, holding out her small hand.

The big woman smiled a toothless smile and put her big arm around Mandie's shoulders.

"I knows who you be. I knows yo' ma," Aunt Pansy told her. Turning to Celia, she added, "I knows this missy's ma, too."

"Hello, Aunt Pansy," Celia greeted her. "I'm glad I got to come back to visit again."

"I sees you didn't bring dat snubby gal wid you dis time," the old woman said.

The girls smiled at each other, knowing Aunt Pansy meant April. "Phoebe, bring dese chillen inside," Aunt

Pansy instructed. She turned to open the screen door.

Inside, Mandie looked around the parlor. The room couldn't possibly hold another piece of furniture. The walls were covered with pictures of people. There was a comfortable, homey look about the room.

"Y'all jes' sits down now. I gotta tell Soony we got mo' comp'ny fo' dinnuh," she said, leaving the room.

Aunt Phoebe plopped down in a nearby rocking chair. "We'se gonna hafta be leavin' soon's we eats," she informed the girls.

Mandie and Celia sat down on the edge of a small settee.

"In that case," Mandie told Celia, "we're going to have to talk to Aunt Pansy during supper."

Celia nodded.

Overhearing the remark, Aunt Phoebe said, "Missies, dis ain't no highfalutin' place like yo' school. We talks all we wants whilst we eats."

"And you won't tell Miss Hope we talked during the meal?" Mandie asked.

" 'Cose not," Aunt Phoebe said. "Y'all be in *my* charge right now. I decides what's propuh. And I says ain't nothin' wrong wid talkin' at de table." She looked up as Aunt Pansy came back through the doorway.

"De vittles is ready," Aunt Pansy announced to her visitors. "Let's go eat." She turned to lead the way into the kitchen.

The room was a combination sitting room and kitchen. A huge fireplace stood at one end, while a shiny, black iron cookstove beamed heat from the far side. In the middle stood a long wooden table covered with a red checked tablecloth and set with plain white dishes. A young Negro girl was taking the food from the pans on the stove.

"Dis heah be Soony," Aunt Pansy told Mandie. "She be my granddaughter. Willie, my son whut lives heah and whut's gone to town right now, is her pa," she explained.

The girls smiled at the young girl who stared curiously at them.

"I'm glad to meet you, Soony," Mandie said, walking over to the stove. "Here, let me help you, Soony," she offered, taking the bowl from the girl and bringing it to the table.

The two old Negro women watched in surprise.

"Thank you, but I kin do it all," Soony said, filling another bowl from a pot on the stove.

"I know you can, but I'd like to help." Mandie stood there waiting for the bowl to be filled. "Makes me feel like I'm back home in my father's log cabin. We had a big room that looked a lot like this one. And I used to have to help with cooking the food, washing the dishes, and milking the cows."

Soony's eyes widened in astonishment. "But, Missy, you goes to dat fine ladies' school," she said.

Mandie took the bowl from her and placed it on the table. "But that's all new to me," Mandie explained. "And I don't really like it. I'd much rather be back home on the farm."

"Well, I nevuh!" Aunt Pansy exclaimed.

As Soony and Mandie finished putting the food on the table, Aunt Pansy gave them a big smile. "Now y'all jes' find a place and sit down. Phoebe, you sit right heah next to me so's we can talk a bit," she said.

Mandie and Celia, determined to talk to Aunt Pansy, sat down as near to her as they could get. Soony sat on the other side of the table next to Aunt Phoebe.

Aunt Pansy cleared her throat. "Befo' we says anothuh word, Phoebe, you ask de blessin'," she said.

They all bowed their heads as Aunt Phoebe prayed.

"We all thanks you, deah Lawd, for dis fine food and all de othuh fine things you gives us. Bless us all and make us mo' bettuh people. Fo' dat we thanks you, deah Lawd. Amen."

"Amen," Aunt Pansy echoed in a loud voice. She reached for the bowl of green beans near her. "Jes' reach and make yo' selfs to home, Missies. We'se all jes' plain people. We jes' takes what we wants."

Mandie picked up the bowl of corn on the cob near her plate, and took out an ear, passing the bowl on to Celia.

The girls piled their plates high with corn, fried chicken, mashed potatoes, green beans, cabbage, cornbread, biscuits, and butter churned right there on the farm. There was a pitcher of cold tea nearby and a huge jug of fresh milk from their cows.

"Aunt Phoebe, you fooled us," Mandie teased. "You said we wouldn't get anything to eat but beans and cornbread, and look at all this food!"

"Now I can't be knowin' whut Soony's goin' to feed us," Aunt Phoebe said. "But I knows fo' sho' theah goin' to be beans and cornbread. Always is."

Everyone laughed.

"Yessum," said Aunt Pansy. "I always has to have mah beans and cornbread. Soony cooked all dis fo' us, an' all de hired hands dey come an' eat latuh, too."

"Aunt Pansy—" Mandie dared to change the subject. "Uncle Cal said you used to work for Mrs. Scott who owned the house before Miss Prudence and Miss Hope made it into a school," she ventured.

"Well, Missy, I sho' did. Aftuh Cal marries Phoebe and

Willie done got hitched with Ella, I gives dem de farm and I moves in wid dat Miz Scott. Dat one nice lady, she wuz," Aunt Pansy said.

"And you stayed with her until she sold the house, didn't you?" Mandie asked.

"Den I stays on to work fo' Miz Prudence and Miz Hope. An' when Cal and Phoebe sells Willie their part of de farm, dey comes to work at de school, and I comes to work fo' de school's farm. Den when Ella dies—dat be Willie's wife—Willie sell his farm, and he come work heah and bring Soony fo' me to raise," the old lady explained.

"Did you know Mrs. Scott's daughter?" Celia asked.

"Which one? She have two daughtuhs," Aunt Pansy said. "Fust one, Missy Helen, she don't belong to de Scotts. Dey 'dopted huh 'cause dey don't be gittin' any chillun. And den, soon as dey gits huh, along come dey own daughtuh, whut dey calls Missy 'Mealya. Sho' is good dey had one theirselfs 'cause dat terrible thing whut happened to Missy Helen."

Mandie and Celia almost dropped their silverware, then leaned forward anxiously.

"What terrible thing, Aunt Pansy?" Mandie asked quickly.

"Lawsy mercy, Missy," the old woman began. "Missy Helen she be promised to dat Mistuh Taylor whut own de nex' farm. Back in dem days de white folks match up dey gals wid some man whut got money. But Missy Helen she don't cater to dat Mistuh Taylor, and she gits huh a sweet-heart whut she say she really luv." Aunt Pansy took a bite of fried chicken and continued. "But dis sweetheart he be young and got no money. So Miz Scott and Mistuh Scott dey forbids huh 'sociatin' wid dis man. Well, if you tells Missy Helen she cain't do sumpin' she gonna do it or else."

Mandie and Celia smiled at each other.

"Then what happened?" Mandie asked, breathlessly.

The old woman wiped her mouth on her apron and continued.

"Lawsy mercy, Missy, dat girl jes' got wiped right outa dis world, fast," the old woman said, her voice breaking with emotion.

"She died?" Mandie asked.

"You bettuh believe she die. Wudn't nothin' left of the po' thing but some ashes," the old woman said, wiping a tear from her eye. "Huh tells me all huh troubles. She meets dis othuh man in a servant's cabin down in de trees 'way from de house 'most ev'y night aftuh ev'ybody go to bed. Den one night de whole cabin burn up. Dey found whut wuz lef' of huh inside. No sign of huh sweetheart."

Celia gasped. "Oh, how horrible!"

"That's so sad, Aunt Pansy," Mandie said. "Did anybody know what caused the fire?"

"No, nevuh did. But right afta dis happened dis Mistuh Taylor sell his farm and move 'way off out wes'. Ain't noboby evuh seed him since," the old woman replied.

"Did they think he might have done it?" Mandie asked.

"Dey wuz 'spicious of him 'cause I tells dem afta it happened what Missy Helen say. She say dat Mistuh Taylor done foun' out she wuz meetin' dis sweetheart, and she say he warned huh to stop it 'cause she be promised ta him. But Missy Helen jes' laugh and keep right on seein' dis sweetheart. Po' girl! She was beautiful, all dat dahk curly hair," the big woman told them.

Mandie's heart beat faster, remembering the girl with dark curly hair whose picture they had found at the cabin site. "Did anyone ever find out who her sweetheart was?" Mandie asked anxiously.

The old woman looked around the table and grunted a time or two. Then looking directly at Mandie, she replied, "Dat still a secret. Ain't nobody but me evuh knowed who he be."

"How did you find out who he was?" Celia asked.

"I seed him one night waitin' at de cabin when I goes by from visitin' ovuh at a friend's house 'cross de creek," Aunt Pansy said.

"Y'all bettuh eat up, Missies," Aunt Phoebe warned the girls. "We'se got to go 'fo' long."

"Aunt Pansy, please tell us who it was," Mandie begged. "We won't tell anybody."

"Now y'all look heah," Aunt Pansy scolded. "Whut fo' you wants to know all dis? Ain't none of it none of yo' bidniss, Missy. It all happen long 'fo' y'all evuh was heerd tell of."

"We have a special reason for wanting to know," Mandie begged. "Please!"

"I ain't nevuh tol' nobody," the old woman said.

Mandie's blue eyes sparkled. "We'll tell you our secret if you'll tell us yours," she offered. "We know about something that I'll bet you knew, too."

"Now whut y'all done be messin' in?" the old woman asked. "I ain't tellin' you 'nuthuh word."

Soony leaned forward. "Come on, Gramma. Ain't fair to stop in de midst of yo' story like dat. We wants to know it all."

Aunt Phoebe tapped her foot impatiently. "So do I. Start sumpin', gotta finish," she said.

The big old woman muttered to herself and continued eating her fried chicken.

"Aunt Pansy, what would you say if we told you we

found the love letters that man wrote to Helen?" Mandie asked.

Aunt Pansy dropped her chicken on her plate and looked at her sharply. "Whut love lettuhs dat be?" she asked.

"The love letters from Helen's sweetheart. We found them and read them all, but there's no name on any of them," Mandie replied. "We also found what's left of the cabin."

"Lawsy mercy! De past done come alive agin!" the old woman exclaimed. "Well, if dey ain't no name on dem lettuhs, den you don't know dey be from Missy Helen's sweetheart. Wheah you find dese lettuhs?"

"In a trunk in the attic. It was locked and we beat the lock open," Mandie answered.

"So dat's whut be in dat trunk," Aunt Phoebe murmured to herself.

Aunt Pansy turned to Phoebe. "Kin I trust dese heah girls?" she asked.

"Sho' kin. Dey awful good at keepin' secrets," Phoebe replied. "I didn't know 'bout dem lettuhs."

The old woman cleared her throat, wiped her fingers on her apron, and looked from Mandie to Celia. "Dis sweetheart, he be named Heathwood—"

"Heathwood?" Mandie exclaimed. "That's Miss Hope's and Miss Prudence's name."

"I knows. He be deah daddy," Aunt Pansy explained. "Y'see, all dis happened long time ago—long, long time ago, 'fo' Mistuh Heathwood evuh marry deah ma. He wuz young, an' worked on a farm down de road. Afta dis happen he pack up and move intuh town. He go to work fo' de railroad, make big money. Den he marry Miz Hope's ma."

"Is he still living?" Mandie asked.

"No, chile. He die right aftuh Miz Hope be bawn," she said.

Aunt Phoebe stood up. "Now we knows de story, we gotta be goin'. It done be dahk outside," she said.

"I puts my trust in y'all not to 'peat anythin' I tol' you," Aunt Pansy told them as everyone else got up from the table.

"Is it all right if we tell Joe? He's my friend from back home in Swain County. He's visiting in Asheville, so he's been helping us solve the mystery," Mandie said.

"Well, I reckons he be all right," Aunt Pansy consented.

"We won't tell anybody else unless it's absolutely, positively necessary, Aunt Pansy," Mandie promised.

"Yes, it might be absolutely, positively necessary," Celia added.

"Well, I don't see wheah no hahm could be, so I reckons I won't hold y'all to no promise not to tell anybody. Jes' y'all be's careful how y'all tells whut I knows. Don't add no extry embrawdery to it," the old woman told the girls. " 'Cause whut I done bin sayin' be's de honest truth."

"Then we can tell anyone we want to?" Mandie asked.

"I s'pose so, but you be's sure you tells it like I tells it," Aunt Pansy warned her.

They promised and said good-bye to the old woman.

On their way back to school, Mandie and Celia discussed this new information. Aunt Phoebe joined in occasionally when she wasn't urging the horse on.

As they rounded a bend in the dirt road the horse suddenly stumbled and came to a standstill, whinnying loudly.

"Whut in de world done happen now?" Aunt Phoebe

said, drawing a sharp breath. "Giddyup, hoss."

But the horse just stood there snorting. When Aunt Phoebe got down to urge him forward, she noticed he was stomping his left front foot. Catching hold of it in the dim moonlight, she felt the hoof and found he had thrown a shoe. No amount of urging could make the horse move.

"He done throwed a shoe, Missies. Guess we gonna hafta leave him heah and walk home. I knows a short cut," she said. "Cal kin come back an' git him."

The girls followed her as she stepped off the road onto a faint path.

Celia gasped. "We're going through the woods!" she said, stopping in her tracks.

"I knows de way. It be fastuh dis way," said the old woman, leading the way.

Mandie took Celia's hand and followed Aunt Phoebe into the woods. The moonlight shone dimly through the trees. They walked on in silence for a while. Then suddenly a big wall loomed up in front of them.

Celia stopped again. "That's the cemetery wall!" she said, shivering.

"We not be goin' in de graveyard, jes' by it," Aunt Phoebe said, trudging on.

Mandie tugged at Celia's hand, forcing her to come along. As they came abreast of the tall wall, the sound of voices reached them. Aunt Phoebe stopped. A shiver went up Mandie's spine, and she felt the hair rise on her head.

Celia squeezed Mandie's hand till it hurt. "Wh-h-hat's th-that?" she cried.

"Ain't nothin'," Aunt Phoebe answered. "Come on."

They each took a step forward. The voices sounded clearer then, evidently coming from behind the graveyard wall.

"I'll take this 'un and you take that 'un," a male voice said.

"That's a fat 'un. This 'un's a pore 'un," said another male voice.

At last Aunt Phoebe looked frightened and she started to run. "Lawsy mercy," she cried, "de Lawd and de Debil's dividin' up de daid!"

The girls broke into a run after her, and the three didn't stop until they came out of the woods at the bottom of the hill below the school. Mandie's side hurt, and she gasped for air. Celia was out of breath, too, and still shivering.

Aunt Phoebe wiped her face with her apron. Her chest heaved up and down from the hard running. "Nevuh . . . in my bawn days . . . has I heerd sech goin's on . . . in a graveyard," she said between breaths. "De end of time . . . must be heah."

Mandie's blue eyes grew wide. "Well, let's get up to the school before it happens, then," she cried.

"Best y'all tell Miz Hope whut happened. I aks Cal to go aftuh de hoss," Aunt Phoebe called to them as she hurried off.

When the girls got back to school, Miss Hope was waiting for them in the alcove.

"Oh, Miss Hope, Miss Hope! God and the Devil are dividing up the dead down in the graveyard!" Celia exclaimed, white as a sheet.

"What!"

"That's what Aunt Phoebe said," Mandie told her, explaining what had happened.

Miss Hope laughed. "That sounds just like Aunt Phoebe. I'm sure there's some good explanation. I don't think God and the Devil would be doing such a thing. I'll get Uncle Cal to check on it. I promise to tell you what he finds out. Now you girls get upstairs. It's almost ten o'clock."

The girls hurried up to their room. As they dressed for bed, they finished putting together all the pieces of their mystery puzzle.

"Well, now we know who the writer of those letters was," said Mandie.

"And what are we going to do?" Celia asked, still shaky.

"We'll have to talk to Joe tomorrow and see what he thinks," Mandie decided.

"*If* the end of the world doesn't come before then," Celia reminded her.

Chapter 12 / Mandie's Regrets

The next morning Miss Hope waited for Mandie and Celia as they came downstairs for breakfast.

"Amanda, Celia, I just wanted to put your minds at ease this morning," the schoolmistress told them in the hallway. "When Uncle Cal went back after the horse and rig last night, he found two boys inside the cemetery dividing up chickens they had stolen. So you see, the end of time hasn't come yet."

"Thank you for letting us know, Miss Hope," Mandie said. "I'm so glad Uncle Cal found them. I hope they're punished for stealing those chickens."

"They probably will be. He knew who they were," Miss Hope replied. "Uncle Cal says the cemetery is overgrown with weeds and brush. I know it's not on our property, but I've sent word to ask the boys from Mr. Chadwick's School to clean it up."

Celia brightened at the mention of Mr. Chadwick's School. "Will Robert Rogers and Thomas Patton be in the group doing the work?" she asked.

Miss Hope looked amused. "That can be arranged, I think. In fact, we'll ask the boys to dinner—just the ones who help with the work."

The girls thanked Miss Hope and hurried on into the dining room.

The hours dragged that day. The girls could hardly wait for Joe to come. At three-thirty, as Joe alighted from Mrs. Taft's buggy, the two girls ran down the steps, grabbed his arms, and hurried him down the hill where they could talk. Sitting on the grass within sight of the school, the three young people spoke excitedly.

"We've found out everything!" Mandie exclaimed.

"Everything?" Joe questioned.

"Absolutely everything!" Celia said, waving her arms.

"Aunt Pansy—that's Uncle Cal's mother—knew everything," Mandie explained.

Together Mandie and Celia repeated Aunt Pansy's story, taking turns telling each detail. Joe sat there taking in every word.

"What a story!" Joe said when they had finished. "But there's just one thing I don't understand. Yesterday you told me about seeing Miss Hope with the rings. I wonder how she got them."

"So do we," Mandie admitted. "Now what should we do?"

"I don't know, but I have to go home tomorrow," Joe said. "It's up to you and Celia now."

"Oh, I wish you could stay here in Asheville for as long as I'm here at this school," Mandie moaned.

"You know that's impossible, Mandie. I have to go home because school will be starting back," he said.

"I sure wish we had a school break to harvest the crops like the country schools do," Celia said.

Joe laughed. "I can see you harvesting crops," he said.

"You aren't gathering in the crops, yourself," Mandie teased.

"That's because we have people living on our farm just to do that. You know that," Joe said. "Anyway, let me know what you do about this whole situation. Write me a note."

"I will," Mandie promised. "I suppose the best thing to do is to just give the letters to Miss Hope. They really belong to her and Miss Prudence, anyway, since their father wrote them."

"You could burn them," Joe suggested.

"No, that would be destroying someone else's property," Mandie reasoned.

"Well, I'd say either give the letters to her or destroy them," Joe advised. "Someone might find them and take them. Remember, someone already discovered those letters in your bureau drawer."

"I think we'll give them to Miss Hope," Mandie decided.

After supper that night, the girls went to Miss Hope's office with the letters.

"We have something that belongs to you," Mandie told the schoolmistress as she and Celia stood before her desk.

"Something that belongs to me?" Miss Hope asked.

Mandie reached forward and put the candy box containing the letters on Miss Hope's desk. Miss Hope looked at the girls and then at the box.

At that moment Miss Prudence walked into the office. "And what have we here?" Miss Prudence asked her sister.

Miss Prudence reached forward and opened the lid, disclosing the letters.

120

"I don't know, Sister," Miss Hope replied, taking an envelope from the box and opening it.

Miss Prudence also picked up a letter, unfolded it, and began reading silently. The two ladies read in unbelief and then looked up at the girls standing before the desk.

"What is this?" Miss Prudence demanded. "Where did you get these?"

"Who wrote these letters?" Miss Hope asked.

"Y'all's father wrote them," Mandie explained.

Miss Hope gasped. "Our father?"

"We found the letters in the attic," Celia added.

Miss Prudence arrogantly shoved the box of letters toward Miss Hope. "Don't include me. He was no father of mine," she snapped.

"My father was not your father?" Miss Hope asked, not understanding.

"You never did know that we had different fathers, did you? My father died when I was a baby and Mother married your father later. Then he gave me his name," Miss Prudence explained.

Miss Hope was overcome. Tears streamed down her face.

Mandie tried to help the situation by explaining. "You see, Miss Hope, your father wrote these letters to Mrs. Scott's daughter, Helen, before he ever knew or married your mother."

Celia cleared her throat. "Since you already have the rings he bought for her, we thought you'd like to have the letters, too," she added.

"Those rings!" Miss Hope exclaimed, bursting into sobs.

Miss Prudence came around the desk and pointed to the door. "Get out of here!" she demanded.

Mandie and Celia, frightened by the outcome, quickly stepped out into the hallway, and Miss Prudence slammed the door behind them.

The two girls turned around quickly, only to find April Snow standing in the hallway.

"So you two are in trouble again, eh?" April laughed.

"Keep out of our business, April!" Mandie said angrily.

"In case you're wondering, I'm the one who put the rings on Miss Hope's desk. They just looked too tempting when I found them in your room, especially after I read those old letters and figured out what y'all were up to," April told them.

"You stole those rings out of our room?" Mandie gasped.

"I didn't steal them. They didn't belong to you," April reasoned. "I had no idea who the owner was, but I knew they weren't yours. I saw you find them out there in the woods at that old cabin. So I took them from your room and put them on Miss Hope's desk."

"Oh, you troublemaker!" Celia snarled.

"Just ignore her, Celia." Mandie tried to calm her friend. "She's just trying to get us to start something. Come on. Let's go to our room."

The two girls hurried up the stairway.

"You've already started something," April called after them.

In their room, the two girls sat on the window seat.

"Celia, we've hurt Miss Hope badly," Mandie said with a shaky voice. "Of all people, I didn't want to hurt Miss Hope."

"But, Mandie, we didn't know all that would happen," Celia said, trying to comfort her. "If Miss Prudence hadn't come in right then, it might not have been so bad. I think

Miss Prudence is really angry with us."

"I know, I know," Mandie said, trying to keep from crying.

"Mandie, it's almost time for the ten o'clock bell. Isn't Uncle Ned coming tonight?" Celia asked.

Mandie straightened up, wiping tears from her eyes.

"That's right," she said. "He *is* coming to see me tonight. I'll tell him what happened. Maybe he can help us straighten everything out."

Later that night, Mandie met the old Indian in the yard. As she told him the whole story, her tears dampened the shoulder of his deerskin jacket.

Uncle Ned listened until she was finished, then smoothed back her long blonde hair, and turned her around to face him. "Papoose, let this be lesson," he said, staring deeply into her eyes. "No make trouble with other people's business. You hurt your friend's heart. Miss Head Lady Number Two your true friend, and you hurt her, Papoose. Must ask forgiveness from Miss Head Lady Number Two. Letters private business of Miss Head Lady Number Two. She not know about father's sweet friend. Remember, I tell you, Papoose—must be careful. Not hurt people."

Mandie looked up into his weather-lined face and with a quivering voice, she said, "I know, Uncle Ned. I'm sorry. I'm so sorry."

"Papoose must think with head first. Then do things," he told her. "Always best not to get in other people's business. Would have been best to leave letters in trunk."

"What should I do, Uncle Ned?" Mandie asked.

"Must ask forgiveness from Miss Head Lady Number Two," the old man said. "Papoose also ask Big God to forgive for hurt to Miss Head Lady Number Two."

Mandie gripped the old man's hand in hers, and turned her face toward the dark sky.

"I'm sorry, dear God," Mandie said, softly. "Please forgive me. Please make me a better person. Lead me down a better path than I've been going lately. Please heal Miss Hope's heart. I'm sorry."

Uncle Ned echoed Mandie's prayer. "Papoose learn lesson, Big God. Not hurt people now. You help, I know, Big God," he concluded.

As they sat there on the bench, Mandie kissed the old man's rough cheek. "I feel better now, Uncle Ned. Tomorrow I'll go straight to Miss Hope and ask her forgiveness," she promised.

"Papoose not forget," the old man said firmly. "I go now. Papoose be good?"

"I promise, Uncle Ned," Mandie replied.

The next afternoon during their free period Mandie and Celia went to Miss Hope's office. Feeling guilty, and afraid of the consequences of their actions, the two girls stood at the doorway until the schoolmistress looked up and saw them. She smiled and waved them inside.

"Sit down, girls," Miss Hope told them. "Mr. Chadwick's boys worked in the graveyard yesterday, and they will finish cleaning it up this afternoon. So we will be expecting them to have supper with us tomorrow night."

"Oh, thank you, Miss Hope, but we came to see you to ask your forgiveness for what we did," Mandie began. "I'm so sorry for my thoughtlessness—more sorry than I can express."

"I'm very sorry too, Miss Hope," Celia confessed. "Please forgive us."

Miss Hope hesitated only a moment. "Of course you're forgiven, girls" she replied. She looked down at the desk.

"I understand. You two are not old enough, I suppose, to realize the shock of everything that happened. And I did give y'all permission to open anything in the attic."

"But, Miss Hope, we're old enough to know better than to go messing in other people's business. We didn't mean to hurt anyone—especially you," Mandie said.

"I know. Maybe it's just as well that everything came out into the open." Miss Hope sighed. "I suppose the biggest shock to me was finding out that my sister is only a half sister to me. But then I should have been told that years and years ago. It wasn't your fault that I didn't know."

"We are sorry, Miss Hope," Celia told her.

"My sister, Miss Prudence, told me the whole story. She knew about everything. I burned all those letters last night and I'm going to sell the rings to the jeweler downtown. It's all over, so let's just forget about it and not mention it anymore," the schoolmistress told them. "Now, about tomorrow night." She changed the subject abruptly. "I've seen to it that Robert and Thomas will be among the group that comes over for supper tomorrow. You girls will want to look your best," she said with a twinkle in her eye.

"We're so grateful to you, Miss Hope, for everything," Mandie said. Standing up, she walked around the desk and gave the surprised schoolmistress a hug. "We love you," she said. Turning quickly, she left the room, and Celia followed. As the two girls approached the stairway Mandie quickly wiped her eyes and smiled at her friend.

"She's a wonderful lady," Mandie declared.

"She certainly is," Celia agreed. "Now we ought to go upstairs and decide what to wear to supper tomorrow night."

"Right," Mandie nodded, "but first I have to write Joe

a letter to let him know what happened. I hope he's not too angry with us."

"I'm sure he'll understand," Celia told her.

The next night, Mandie wore her pale blue voile dress with rows and rows of frills around the full skirt. She left her long blonde hair swinging freely around her shoulders. Around her neck hung the tiny gold locket containing pictures of her mother and father.

Celia's dress was lemon-colored, edged with lace and black velvet ribbon. She tied her auburn curls with a matching black ribbon.

When Mr. Chadwick's boys arrived in the parlor, Robert and Thomas eagerly sought the girls out.

"It's been a long time," Thomas said, coming to stand before Mandie.

"Please sit down," Mandie invited.

"It's been too long," Robert told Celia as he and Thomas joined the two girls on the settee.

"I'm glad to see you, Robert." Celia blushed.

"It was awfully nice of you boys to clean up that old cemetery. I'm sure all those dead people would thank you if they could, but we want to especially thank you," Mandie said.

The girls related the events of their stormy afternoon in the cemetery and their recent experience with Aunt Phoebe.

"So you see, we're very thankful for your work," Mandie concluded.

"I'm glad, Mandie," Tommy replied. "Because now that we have done you a favor, you must do us a favor."

As if on cue, Robert invited Celia to go for a stroll in the yard, giving Mandie and Tommy a chance to talk alone. "My parents have asked me to invite you and your parents for a visit to our home," Tommy began. "We'll be having some holidays before long, and my parents would like to know if y'all can come to Charleston then."

"Oh, Tommy, thank you," Mandie replied. "I'll write to my mother right away and let you know what she says. I'm so anxious to see the ocean."

"I'd like to show you the whole city of Charleston, too," Tommy said. "There isn't another place like it in the world."

"I can't wait to see it all," Mandie assured him. "I'll write to my mother tonight."

Later that night, as the ten o'clock bell rang for lights out, Mandie was just finishing the letter to her mother as she promised.

Mandie told her mother all about the letters she and Celia had found in the trunk, the rings, the tumbled-down cabin, and what they had done about it. She explained that she and Celia had learned their lesson and were doing their best to stay out of trouble.

Then she told her mother about Tommy and his parents' invitation to visit them in Charleston. She begged her mother to accept the invitation, reminding her that her daughter had never seen the ocean.

Would her mother agree to this trip which Mandie wanted so much? Would she think Mandie deserved this after the trouble she had stirred up?

Mandie prayed about it that night and asked God to let her go if He saw fit. That was all she could do. She went to sleep that night dreaming of the ocean.